✓ P9-BZN-305

GIRL OF KOSOVO

DELL YEARLING BOOKS are designed especially to entertain and enlighten young people. Patricia Reilly Giff, consultant to this series, received her bachelor's degree from Marymount College and a master's degree in history from St. John's University. She holds a Professional Diploma in Reading and a Doctorate of Humane Letters from Hofstra University. She was a teacher and reading consultant for many years, and is the author of numerous books for young readers.

ALICE MEAD

Girl of Kosovo

A DELL YEARLING BOOK

The author gratefully acknowledges Dr. Steven L. Burg,
Professor of Politics, Brandeis University,
for his critical reading of the manuscript.

Published by
Dell Yearling
an imprint of
Random House Children's Books
a division of Random House, Inc.
1540 Broadway
New York, New York 10036

Visit us on the Web! www.randomhouse.com/kids

**Educators and librarians, for a variety of teaching tools, visit us at
www.randomhouse.com/teachers**

ISBN: 0-440-41853-4

Reprinted by arrangement with Farrar, Straus and Giroux

Printed in the United States of America

February 2003

10 9 8 7 6 5 4 3

OPM

FOR ALBIN

PLACE-NAMES

ALBANIAN	SERBIAN
Kosova	Kosovo
Deçan	Decani
Drenicë	Drenica
Fushë Kosovë	Kosovo Polje
Gjakovë	Djakovica
Gllogovc	Glogovac
Malishevë	Malisevo
Mitrovicë	Mitrovica
Pejë	Pec
Prishtinë	Pristina
Prizren	Prizren

For nearly five hundred years, much of the Balkan peninsula of southeast Europe was under the rule of the vast Ottoman (Turkish) Empire. When the Ottoman Empire collapsed around 1900, European leaders drew new borders. By 1913, the country of Albania had been created. Its boundaries left half of the ethnic Albanian population in the neighboring country of Yugoslavia, in a province called Kosovo.

Yugoslavia was made up of six republics: Serbia, Croatia, Macedonia, Slovenia, Bosnia and Herzegovina, and Montenegro. From 1945 to 1980, it was ruled by a dictator named Tito. Tito managed to hold the six republics together, but all the while power struggles were simmering below the surface among the many ethnic groups, including the Serbs and the Kosovar Albanians.

From 1913 to 1998, Kosovo was, for the most part, subjugated by Serbian rule. For the Serbs, Kosovo was the historic cradle of their culture. It was also a strategically located province, rich in minerals. For the Albanians, who came to make up 90 percent of the population, it was home—and one of the poorest, most undeveloped regions in Europe.

In 1987, seven years after Tito's death, an authoritarian Serb leader, Slobodan Milosevic, rose to power. Nationalist pride had now become a major force in Yugoslavia. Each population no longer identified itself first as Yugoslavian but in Kosovo, for example, as Albanian or Serbian. They did not trust each other or believe that they could share a future together.

To demonstrate that the Serbs were the most powerful group in Yugoslavia, in 1989 Milosevic established emergency law in Kosovo. Large numbers of Serbian military police and tanks had been in the region since 1981, when Albanian students and others began to demonstrate for Kosovo's independence. Now Milosevic sent more, to control the nearly two million Albanians and to squelch their quest for independence. Milosevic suppressed the Albanians with his harsh military rule.

After nearly ten years of beatings, widespread imprisonments, joblessness, poverty, deprivation of civil rights, and poor medical care, the Albanians intensified their rebellion. The center of the effort was based in the Drenica farming region west of Pristina. That was where the Kosovo Liberation Army (KLA) started.

The KLA was formed for two reasons: to protect Albanians from the brutality of Serb police in the villages, and to liberate Kosovo from Serbia. By 1998 other republics of the former Yugoslavia had successfully broken away from Serbia and formed their own countries. Now the Albanians demanded self-determination. The Serbs refused to give them independence. War was inevitable.

Beginning in March 1998, the first phase of the war was fought by the Serb army and police and the KLA. It ended in October 1998, when the United States negotiated a cease-fire.

During those five months, hundreds of villages had been attacked by the Serb army, driving over 300,000 unarmed civilians into the woods and hills to hide for weeks at a time.

After the October cease-fire, Western nations insisted that the Serbs withdraw their army from Kosovo and let international peacekeepers establish order there. President Milosevic did not want the KLA to take advantage of the situation, so he moved in more troops and tanks.

Leaders of the North Atlantic Treaty Organization gave Milosevic a deadline of March 23, 1999, to remove his troops or face bombing. Again he refused. Milosevic did not believe NATO would bomb his country.

On March 24, 1999, NATO, led by the U.S. Air Force, started an eleven-week bombing campaign to force Serb troops to leave Kosovo. This was the second phase of the war in Kosovo. During the NATO bombing, Albanian villagers were again brutally attacked by the Serb army. Although the numbers are uncertain, it is believed that approximately 11,000 people died. Over 3,000 are still missing. About 800,000 people fled into neighboring countries. President Milosevic was declared a war criminal for his brutal ethnic-cleansing policies.

The war ended on June 9, 1999, and the United Nations set up a three-year protectorate government in Kosovo with NATO troops (called KFOR) as peacekeepers. Sadly, this temporary halt to violence did little to resolve the basic conflict. The future of Kosovo is still far from certain, as the Albanians continue to dream of independence, and nationalist Serb leaders declare they will retake Kosovo.

GENEROSITY IS THE FIRST
STEP TOWARD PEACE.

—*Buddhist saying*

GIRL OF KOSOVO

I loved our village life. I loved our farm and the apple orchard. I had my friends at school, and at home I did chores—helping with the cow, fetching water, bringing in firewood. It was an honor for me to serve tea to my father and his friends, like Mehmet Bagu, the beekeeper. He was old, and my father respected him very much. Mehmet gave us honey made from apple blossoms.

My best friend, Lena Goran, lived next door, just up the lane, although we didn't see each other much anymore. Lena's family was Serb, and mine, Albanian. "Zana," my Uncle Vizar told me a few years ago, "you shouldn't play with her." I didn't like him very much.

I was used to the Serb police, stopping us in the roads and shops, searching the boys' backpacks when we walked to school. The police had always been there. I didn't pay any attention to them really, although I knew enough not to speak at all around them. That was because I couldn't speak Serbian very well.

But the way I remember it now, everything changed on one day. It was the day of the Serbian New Year, January 6, 1998. I was eleven. Mama, my fifteen-year-old brother, Ilir, and I had taken the bus to Prishtinë, our capital, to sell eggs at the street market by the soccer stadium. Luckily, my other two brothers, Luan and Burim, stayed home.

That day there were police everywhere in the marketplace. Some were in uniform, some in everyday clothes—but even without any uniforms, you could still tell they were police because of how big and muscular they were.

They were taking money from people. A few were drunk, probably because it was their New Year's and they had been celebrating with lots of beer. They took whatever they wanted from the Albanian farmers who had come to town—watches, fruit, anything. I guess Milosevic, the Serb leader, didn't pay them enough, so they had to take from us Albanians.

An old man, a villager wearing a traditional white felt hat, began to yell at them. "You have no right to bully us like this!" he shouted. "You're no better than thieves!"

The police grabbed his arm and twisted it up high behind his back. The street was packed with people. But now everyone stepped back, and a space cleared around the old man. I was standing at the edge of the circle and could see everything.

They twisted his arm up so high that he stood on his tiptoes. Then they began to beat him in front of everybody. They punched his stomach. He tried to bend over, but he couldn't. Four of them were beating him. One took out his club and cracked it against the side of the old man's head near his eye. Blood began to flow.

The Albanian men in the crowd did nothing to help. No one dared to move or even speak. We all watched in silence. We knew that anyone who tried to help would be arrested.

Finally, after about five minutes, the police let go and the old man dropped to the ground. He lay hunched up in a mud puddle. They kicked him, but not that hard, and told him to go to Albania. Then they left with their German marks and food.

Ilir whispered to me, "Someday I'll kill them for this. I will never allow them to forget what they've done to us."

I looked at him in surprise.

"I will. Don't you believe me?" he asked more loudly.

"Shut up!" I whispered. "What if someone hears you?"

But that was only the beginning of our trouble. By afternoon, the bus station was full of police and soldiers in long, brown wool coats over their camouflage uniforms. Compared to the police, the soldiers looked so young. They were boys, really, with pink cheeks and ears. Not much older than Ilir.

In the crowd waiting for the buses, I saw Lena and her mother. I waved hi to Lena when no one was looking, and she grinned. I knew my mother and Mrs. Goran wouldn't speak. There were only three Serb families in our village. Most Serbs lived in Malishevë or Mitrovicë or Fushë Kosovë.

Lena and her mother stood at the head of the line and boarded the bus first. When we got on, three policemen did, too. One sat in the very first seat behind the driver. The other two sat way in the back. Lena and her mom sat in the middle, two rows in front of us.

It would take us over an hour to reach our little village in the Drenicë region. We lived just past the town of Gllogovc.

We had gone only a few kilometers when the bus was stopped at a large police roadblock in Fushë Kosovë, a Serbian village on the outskirts of Pristinë. Well, we Albanians called it Fushë Kosovë, which meant Field of Kosova. The Serbs called it Kosovo Polje, or the Field of Blackbirds. In Kosova, there are two names for all the towns.

The policemen began to walk slowly down the aisle of the bus, checking everyone's identification cards. "IDs.

Here, hand it over. What's in that bag? Open it. Good. Next. You—where's your ID?"

They were looking for weapons. Each policeman took out a knife and used it to poke through the bags and under the seats. They even stabbed at the ugly brown bus curtains to see if anything was hidden there. But what could be hidden in those short little curtains? They did it to scare us.

All this time, no one spoke. The bus windows were steamed up from everyone's breath. I tried to ignore the approaching police by drawing funny faces in the steam. In the old days, when Lena and I were together constantly, we played ticktacktoe on the bus windows. Now I couldn't even talk to her in public.

Without thinking, I wrote my name with my finger, Zana Dugolli, but quickly erased it so the police wouldn't see any Albanian words. Zana means "nectar" or "magic one."

When they got to us, they stared at Ilir too long. My heart thumped. Could they somehow have overheard the angry words he had whispered to me in the marketplace? That wasn't possible, was it?

Ilir blushed and stared at the back of the seat in front of him. Mama sat next to him, looking completely calm, her hands quietly folded on her bag.

They picked up our shopping bags and searched them. Then one said to Ilir, "How old are you?"

"Fifteen," he answered in Serbian. They would have beaten him for sure if he had answered in Albanian. All the people on the bus held their breath, sensing trouble. The police studied Ilir's ID card.

"Hmm. You live near Glogovac?"

"Yes."

"Do you know Adem Jashari?" he asked casually.

"No."

"No? Of course you do. Where does he live?"

"I don't know."

Those were lies. We all knew Adem Jashari, at least we all knew of him. He lived in Prekaz, another small village in the Drenicë region, and was the leader of a new secret army called the Kosova Liberation Army, which had killed some Serb policemen during the past year. Every Albanian child knew that.

The policeman grabbed Ilir's arm. "Come on. Get off the bus."

He pulled Ilir, making him scramble over Mama. Mama got up, too, and followed them down the aisle so that Ilir wouldn't be alone with the police.

Would they beat him? I knew they had taken him because of his age. Now they would call him a terrorist and say he was bringing weapons for the KLA. And the terrible part was that my father and my Uncle Vizar had joined the KLA two weeks before. It was supposed to be a secret from us kids, but we all knew. In a village like ours, there were no real secrets.

By now I was crumpling up with fear. My heart felt tight and I was crying inside, but I didn't make a sound. Why had we ever bothered to go to Prishtinë to sell a few eggs? The moments dragged by.

I couldn't bear sitting and waiting. I had to find out what was happening. So I got to my feet and went to the front of the bus. The police had pulled the driver off as well, and the bus door was open. They had taken Ilir and Mama into a large shed by the side of the road. Meanwhile, two other policemen were questioning the driver. They made him open the compartments under the bus so they could look for weapons there. I hesitated by the door.

An old woman in one of the front seats caught hold of my puffy ski jacket and tugged me back inside. "Stay here," she whispered. "Your mother doesn't need two children to worry about. Go sit down now. Everything will be all right. Go!"

I knew she was right. If I got off, too, that would only make things worse for everyone. But it was agony to feel so helpless. I was powerless to help my brother, just as we had all been powerless to help the old man at the market this morning. Ducking my head, I blinked back tears as I hurried to my seat.

When she saw me pass by crying, Lena's mother immediately got up and got off the bus. I peeked out the window as she entered the shed. Lena turned around in her seat and gave me a tiny smile. Maybe her mother would tell the soldiers and police to leave Ilir alone.

And then, suddenly, Mama and Ilir were back, edging their way up the aisle, followed by Lena's mother. The driver was back, too. He shut the door, and the bus lurched forward. The police took their seats. No one spoke. I looked at my mother, but she sat as still and calm as ever, her hands folded as quietly as two round stones.

T W O

Our village consisted of about twenty houses, small farms like ours with chickens, a cow, and apple orchards.

The bus drove slowly through Gllogovc and Poklek, until it finally stopped at the turnoff to our village. From there we had to walk up a long, sloping hill. Mr. Goran had driven down to the main road to pick up Lena and her mother and drive them home. But he didn't offer us a ride. It wouldn't look good if he did, and, if we accepted, the whole village would talk about us behind our backs and call us traitors.

We started the long walk, carrying our grocery bags. Although my mittens helped, the bag handles soon cut into my palms. But this wasn't a good day to complain, so I said nothing. Instead, I hurried to keep up with Mama and Ilir.

The minute we got home, I asked, "Mama, what did Lena's mother say to the police?"

"Nothing, Miss Big Ears. Now go get water for tea, Zana," Mama said to me as she unpacked the flour, oil, sugar, bitter coffee, and cookies. "Ilir, bring in some more firewood. It's getting late."

I took a pan from the wood stove and hurried back out into the cold, crisp air. I was glad to be home. The air in Prishtinë smelled of diesel fumes and bitter smoke from piles of smoldering garbage. I was a country girl. When Albanian kids in Prishtinë made fun of us village kids and called us "stupid peasants," I didn't care. They didn't know what they were missing in their noisy city full of boutiques and disco bars. As far as I was concerned, city kids were a bunch of snobs.

Our house stood near the crest of the hill. All around us was a view of woods, valleys, and rolling hills, with the steep Albanian mountains to the west. It was a beautiful spot, and once Lena told me it was the reason her family had moved here from Mitrovicë. Her father had hated the city.

But it was cold out now, and the ground near the pump was frozen with hard, lumpy mud. Quickly I pumped water into the big pan. I hadn't bothered to put my mittens back on, and the pump handle felt ice-cold.

Once Luan, who was twelve, had spit on his palm and grabbed the handle. And then his hand stuck to the pump handle, and my mother had to pour warm water on it so he could get his hand loose. Luan was always doing things like that.

I hurried back inside and was greeted by the smell of simmering french fries. Mama was slicing big chunks of homemade bread, and I cut white cheese into slabs. We would have bread, cheese, potatoes, and glasses of tea for dinner.

I carried the food into the living room and set it on the low table. The boys were watching auto racing from Italy on TV. Bright yellow and red cars covered with advertisements whizzed around a curvy racetrack. I couldn't see anything interesting about it at all.

My father sat down in the big chair. My mother served him first. He took a piece of bread and tore it in two. "So you had a big scare on the bus today?" he asked.

I nodded. "I hate them," I said.

Papa sighed, then leaned forward and looked at me closely. "Listen, Zana, don't let them fill your heart with hate. Whatever happens. Promise me that. Will you?"

But I paid no attention, except to the words "whatever happens." Those words scared me. What was going to happen? Did he mean to say "when a war started"?

My father took the TV remote and switched to the Albanian station from Tirana, the only place that broadcast

13

news about our situation. We found out that two Serbian police stations had been attacked the night before—one in Pejë and one near the border with Serbia, in Mitrovicë. Some KLA members had fired automatic rifles at police standing in front of the police stations, and one Serb had been killed. That was why there had been so many police around today. And now their leaders would once again call us terrorists on Serbian TV from Belgrade.

I started to chew on my fingernails.

My mother noticed me fretting. "Zana," Mama said, "bring in more water for the dishes. And make the tea."

I didn't want to go out again and leave my family, now that we were all sitting together.

Luan, only one year older than I was, realized it immediately. "Yeah, Zana," Luan teased. "Get more water."

I wanted to smack him. Grinning, he watched me to see if I would. If I tried, I knew he would grab my wrist and twist it. He was suddenly much stronger than I was, and I didn't like that one bit. So I glared at him and stuck out my tongue instead. Let him try to grab that!

"Quiet down, Luan, unless you're interested in going for water yourself," Papa said calmly.

On my way out, I gave Papa a big hug. I loved my father. He was always so fair with all of us. Mama spoiled the two younger boys.

But the awful day wasn't over. Outside, as I hurried past the small stone stable where we kept our cow and two goats, I suddenly heard a rapid burst of machine-gun fire rattle across the fields and echo in the hills. It wasn't close. Maybe it was from Poklek down the hill.

I grabbed the pump handle. As the water splashed into the pan, I heard it again—another rapid burst breaking the silence of our valley. I picked up the pan too quickly, spilling some of the icy water on my slippers. I heard a third burst as I hurried up the steps and into the kitchen.

Now I knew that they were shooting because one of their policemen had been killed. We would all pay heavily. It didn't matter to the Serbs who had killed their policeman. All Albanians would suffer for the actions of one. That was just how it was.

Making the tea was my job. Mama had bought a lemon today in Prishtinë and some sugar. I got four little tea glasses and tiny spoons ready on the tray. My little brother, Burim, who was only eight, and I wouldn't have any. Then I cut the lemon into lots of little wedges.

Suddenly, outside, my Uncle Vizar's dog, a small tan-and-white collie, barked. I froze and listened. Someone was nearby. It couldn't be soldiers or police, could it?

My father had heard the dog barking, too. He quickly went to the door and looked out.

I knew where he kept his gun. It was under his dirty old farm jacket, hanging on a peg near the door. He had gotten it in Prizren from a man who'd smuggled it in from Albania. It wasn't new or anything. It was old and battered-looking. The gunstock was wrapped in duct tape to hold it together. Papa had dug a hole someplace in the orchard, where he could hide the gun in case our house was searched. He had always told us he would never own a gun. And now he had one, a Kalashnikov rifle.

Having a gun scared me. If a group of twenty soldiers came and searched the house, how could our father protect us? And if they found the gun, they would take Papa to prison and torture him for days. Maybe they would even shoot him on the spot. They were allowed to kill terrorists that way, without a trial or anything. Calling Albanians terrorists gave them the right to kill us anytime they wanted to.

I set the pan on the stove and put in another log. Papa opened the door and stood on the top step. Then Uncle Vizar appeared. He had come to visit from his house across the lane. His wife, Aunt Sevdie, was Mama's sister.

"Good evening, Hasan," he said to my father, giving him a cigarette. "Sounds like they're everywhere tonight. All the roads in and out of Prishtinë are blocked."

I went to the doorway and leaned my head against my father. He put his arm around my shoulders, while we listened to the gunfire echoing through the hills.

"They took Ilir off the bus today at Fushë Kosovë," my father said. "Why take a young boy like that? Just to show off, I guess. It doesn't mean anything. Come in, Vizar, and have some tea with us."

I got another glass for Uncle Vizar. I picked up the tray and carried it into the living room. Burim was cuddled against my mother.

They'd all heard the gunshots by now. Trying to pretend we had a normal life, Ilir and Luan were watching a soap opera from Venezuela. It was in Spanish, with Serbian subtitles, and Ilir was fooling around, reciting lines he'd learned from watching the same show so many times.

"Bernardo, you have betrayed me!" Ilir cried out, clutching at his heart. "I trusted you. I gave you my love, and you betrayed me!"

"*Buenos días,*" Luan said so Ilir wouldn't get all the attention. "*Buenas noches. Hasta la vista,* baby!" That was from an American movie. Luan could be such an idiot at times.

I put the tray on the low table and handed the men their glasses first. Just as they began to sip the hot tea, the TV went blank and the lights went out. Quickly Mama flicked on her cigarette lighter and went to find some candles.

We all sat in the candlelight, listening to the gunshots that went on and on.

I got up and poured more tea for my father and Uncle Vizar. Without the soap opera to make fun of, no one had anything to say.

"Papa, will the police come here?" Luan asked finally.

"Of course not. They just want to scare us, so don't be afraid, eh, Luan? You'll only make them happy that way." He gave Luan's knee a little squeeze.

"But why did they question Ilir?" he asked.

"Ilir? Because of his muscles," Papa said to make us smile.

Burim curled up in Mama's lap like a big baby. I was jealous of him because I wanted to be there, too. We all still believed that our parents could keep us safe.

"Well," said Uncle Vizar, "I'd better go. Thank you for the tea, Zana. You're a good hostess. Don't see me out. I've got a lighter with me."

But Mama said, "Zana, take this candle and go with him so he can see to tie his boots."

We always wore slippers in the house and left our boots and shoes by the back door.

Cupping the flame with my hand, I led the way down the dark hall and held the candle high while my uncle bent to tie his bootlaces.

"How's Ardi?" I asked.

Ardi, my cousin, was eleven years old. We were friends, now that I didn't have Lena to play with anymore. But if I played with Ardi, that made Luan jealous. He wanted Ardi for himself.

"Fine. He's playing Nintendo all the time, as always."

But now that the lights were out, he probably wasn't playing anything. He would be sitting in the dark, sick at heart, just the way Luan and I were. And what would Lena and her family be doing, listening to all that gunfire?

After Uncle Vizar had gone, we pulled the sofa beds out and put the pillows and blankets on them. Without the TV, there was no reason to stay awake, wasting the candles.

Being the two youngest, Burim and I shared one sofa bed. Luan and Ilir each had their own. In minutes, Burim forgot all about the shootings in the valley and fell asleep. But not me. I tossed and turned, remembering our trip to the market, how the police beat the old man, how Ilir had been pulled off the bus, how Papa's Kalashnikov hung under the old jacket by the door.

Was a war really starting here? The Serbs said they would kill us just as they had killed the Bosnians before us. Kosova was theirs and for Serbs only, they said, even though most of the people living here were Albanians. They wanted us all to leave.

And now, because people in the villages had gotten tired of ten years of beatings and searches, and the KLA had fought back, they called us all terrorists.

But Papa said we weren't terrorists at all. The truth was, he said, that we lived in a great big concentration camp, and every day the police beat us and stole from us, and we could do nothing to protect ourselves. He said terrorists were people who caused terror, and that the KLA was trying to keep us safe.

Here in the villages, we were already poor—yet they took our money, jewelry, TVs, even our food. What more did the Serbs want? Why did they hate us and want us dead?

My father was a good man, always so kind and fair with us kids. We had Serb neighbors right here, and never had there been a problem between us, although we now kept to ourselves for the most part. But that wasn't a crime, was it? And today Lena's mother had helped us at the checkpoint, because she still remembered when Lena and I had been little girls together.

Then I thought about the gunshots again. We had been in danger for years, for my whole life. Why didn't the world come to help us? Who would save us if a war did start?

Thoughts like these were the reason I couldn't sleep.

Early in the gray January dawn I woke up. My left arm was numb and tingly, and I needed to go to the bathroom, but I didn't want to rush outside in my pajamas, so I huddled deeper under the heavy blanket instead.

I heard my father in the kitchen, putting fresh logs in the stove. And then I heard him go out. I waited a minute or two before I got up and tiptoed into the kitchen. I pulled back the heavy jacket. The beat-up old Kalashnikov rifle was gone.

THREE

Strangely enough, after that one awful day, life seemed to calm down again. There were no new KLA attacks, and there seemed to be fewer police around. We had a big, soggy wet snowstorm, and we stayed home from school and played outside for hours, using pieces of old cardboard to slide down the steep hills. I hoped that because of the snow, Lena would come out. But she didn't, and I felt bad about that.

When I stopped to think, I felt strange, as if my head were splitting in two. I couldn't decide what was real. Was that awful day of the shootings and the beating the way it would always be for us? Or would life go on as it had before? Maybe it hadn't been so bad, after all.

Whenever I drove myself crazy thinking about what might happen, I ran across the street and played with

Ardi's Nintendo. Most of the time, Luan had beaten me to it.

But in the first few days of March, we saw on the news that Serb forces had attacked some nearby villages early in the morning. They killed Adem Jashari and fifty-four members of his family, then burned down their houses. They shot the women and children, uncles, cousins—everybody. Only a girl my age was found alive. She was hiding under a table, too afraid to go for help. The Jashari family was destroyed.

The photos of all the bodies—shot, stiff and lifeless, eyes wide open and staring, wrapped in bloody blankets—appeared on Albanian TV.

So now the KLA had lost its leader. I figured Milosevic thought that would put a stop to our resistance, and that now we would all leave and go to Albania, which was what the Serbs wanted.

Although all the roads were blocked by the police so no one could drive anywhere, Albanian villagers from all over walked through the hills and fields to attend the mass burial. My father and old Mehmet put on their suits and ties and set off walking. They came back after dark.

My father sat at the kitchen table, eating beans and bread. "There will be war," he said. "Everyone says so. Listen. From now on, I want you kids to sleep in your clothes."

Mama only nodded. She didn't seem surprised at all. There was no doubt in anybody's mind that this was the start of war. But no one knew exactly how it would happen. We simply waited. And falling asleep became harder than ever.

Two days after the funeral, Uncle Vizar got some gasoline and two new spark plugs and started his beat-up old 1986 Lada, which had been sitting under an apple tree for two years. While the engine sputtered and warmed up, huge puffs of smoke came out the tailpipe. He had been using the car as a doghouse for their collie, so he had to sweep off the broken seats a little before we could get in.

He took Luan, Burim, Ardi, and me to see the ruins of the Jashari house.

"For Albanians this is now a historic site," he proudly told us. "Here our fight for freedom has begun. Adem Jashari is our first martyr. He gave his life for our freedom, and we will never let them forget it. They cannot drive us out of Kosova no matter what they do."

"KLA! KLA!" Luan and Ardi chanted. "KLA! KLA!"

I glared at them. What show-offs, acting like soldiers.

We got out of the car and stood in the mud. Immediately, I felt scared. Not much was left of the Jashari house. A row of noisy black birds perched on the blackened cinder blocks. The roof tiles had collapsed, and the windows were all shattered. Every bit of furniture was burned to ashes.

The police had burned their tractor and cars. On the walls, they had spray-painted in black paint the Serbian cross with the four "S" symbols. And a swollen dead cow lay on its side in a pile of hay. When I saw the cow, I thought I would be sick. I hurried back to the car and sat inside, waiting for Uncle Vizar and the boys.

I hated my uncle for bringing us here. Did he think this would inspire us? I didn't want to be in a war. A war was just smashing things, ruining everything. Why did he sound so proud, talking about it, as if he himself had done something good, when in fact he'd done nothing?

Why did everyone think that shooting and killing would make us free? Why did the Serbs think that, as well? I couldn't understand it, but it seemed everyone felt that way except for me. Was there something wrong with me?

I looked out the car window at the blackened walls, the gaping hole where an orange-tiled roof had been, at the hundreds of bullet casings lying in the trampled mud in the yard. I had an imagination. I could imagine what happened here—the screaming and begging not to be shot. With my head resting on the window, I started to cry. This farm could have been ours. Their cow looked just like ours. The Jasharis weren't free at all. They were dead. All except that one girl, and what kind of life did she have now?

How could a bunch of farmers fight the whole Serb army? If they were going to shoot at our houses with tanks, it was hopeless. We could never survive that.

Finally Uncle Vizar and the boys got back in the car. "Did you see the cow?" Ardi asked me in a low voice. "Wasn't it terrible?"

I nodded. Even Luan stayed quiet for a few moments.

We left the Jasharis' house and drove to a big field where all the bodies were buried in a long row. I could see mound after mound of fresh earth heaped on the graves. Several modern cars, BMWs and Jeeps, were parked there. They had white press-pass cards in the windows.

Reluctantly, I got out of the car and dragged up the hill, following my uncle. Luan and Ardi ran ahead like two ghouls from an American horror movie. They were crazy and stupid, I decided. I wasn't going to play with them anymore. And since I didn't have Lena to play with, I would never play with anyone again. It would be better that way.

The sky was overcast and gray. Low tattered clouds ripped to pieces above my head. The ground was soggy from a recent shower. I could see bits of pale green grass in the trodden ground beneath my feet. How could spring come if there was going to be a war here?

My uncle and the boys walked slowly past each grave. I stood and watched them from a distance. Each grave was draped with the red Albanian flag, so they all looked the same. The foreign reporters crouched beside different graves, taking snapshots. I felt bitter and angry when I saw them doing that.

How was it that foreigners could come take pictures of us when we were dead, but couldn't come to help us stay alive? I wanted to let the air out of their fancy tires so they would be stuck here, trapped the way we were. Maybe the Serbs would kill them, too, when the time came.

If there was a war, we'd all end up the same, rows of dead bodies with names on sticks. All Albanians would be terrorists. All Serbs would be criminals and murderers. That was the way it would be. And despite what Uncle Vizar said about being martyrs and heroes and wanting to die for the cause of a free Kosova, I knew I didn't want to die. I just wanted to live.

That was the problem. My problem.

I turned and went back to the car. I sat there, wondering what family the Serbs would attack next, while the world watched the slaughter on CNN and Euronews.

FOUR

After the massacre, the weeks passed, oddly quiet. It was a soggy, cold spring with a lot of rain. But somehow, even with the heavy clouds, the daffodils came up and bloomed. Lena's mother loved daffodils and had planted a whole bed of them near the back door. Down on the highway and in Gllogovc, every day we saw more and more police and personnel carriers.

Then one morning in mid-April, I awoke before dawn to the sound of ear-shattering explosions. They seemed to be coming from everywhere. I sat up, confused. I couldn't figure out what I was hearing. The crashing noises came again, explosions so strong that they shook my ribs and vibrated in my heart and teeth.

There was a shrill whistling sound. A mortar shell glanced off our roof and struck the yard below, exploding there and spattering dirt and rock against the windows. Still in bed, Burim and I clung together, screaming for our father.

"Ilir, Zana, Burim, Luan!" my father shouted. "Grab your boots and a blanket. Hurry! We have to leave!"

I heard bursts of machine-gun fire, close now. The bullets were spraying the outside wall of the house. Thank God we were already dressed.

Whimpering and shaking, I grabbed my boots and Burim's, and followed Luan into the kitchen. My father dashed outside for the tractor and wagon. My mother was frantically gathering up food and shoving it all in bags. Ilir ran in with our coats, and we pulled them on as best we could. We didn't dare turn on the lights, and the sun hadn't risen yet.

Suddenly the shooting stopped, and there was complete silence, as though the air had frozen solid. We stood still, confused. But then we heard screams from farther up the lane near the top of the hill. I turned to Mama.

"Have the police gone?" I asked. "Is it over?"

"No. Quick. Go. Get in the wagon. Luan, you lift Burim. Zana, take the bags of food. Hurry!"

She pushed all of us out the door. I turned for one more look at our house, and for some reason, I could see through Mama's nightgown and unbuttoned coat that she was pregnant. Why had no one told me, I wondered. Did Ilir already know?

In my confusion, I dropped one of the bags of food and stumbled on the end of the blanket. I left it lying in the mud.

Papa was there with the tractor and wagon. Luan and Burim piled in the front of the wagon, and we threw the food in after them. Then Ilir and I got in, with Mama at the back. The tractor lurched forward.

We could see our neighbors running in terror down the lane, parents stumbling as they tried to carry the littlest children, who clung to their necks, crying. To the left, up the hill, were billows of smoke from where barns and houses had caught fire.

Papa started to drive the tractor into the lane. And then it happened. I heard a sharp whistle, as though air were ripping in front of us, and then a blinding explosion forced a blast of air right into my face. I was already screaming and trying to cover my eyes. Bits of hard, sharp pieces flew everywhere. Luan and Burim were hit. They crumpled forward and fell out of the wagon. My father and the tractor were destroyed.

My mother was screaming as she jumped to the ground. She ran forward and grabbed my father. But we could all see that he was dead. She turned to Luan and Burim. Burim, too, had been destroyed by the blast. I can't describe his body.

The engine of the tractor was on fire.

But Luan was still alive, lying on the ground. He

stared at me desperately. Quickly I jumped down next to him, but I couldn't stand. My leg collapsed. My boot was gone, and so was the bottom half of my sweatpants. My foot hung dangling from my leg. My other leg gave way and I lay on the ground, screaming. Ilir knelt by my side.

Our neighbors saw we had been badly hurt. One man picked me up. Another tore Mama away from Burim. Uncle Vizar picked up Luan, and they ran with us down the lane to the school.

But Luan's arms hung down, loose and heavy. His eyes were now closed.

"Wait!" Uncle Vizar called. "I'll leave him here in this cellar. We'll come back for him. Ilir, give me that blanket."

"No!" I screamed. "Don't leave him!"

I could see that Luan was unconscious. When he woke up alone in that awful cellar, he'd be terrified. I hated Uncle Vizar.

But no one paid any attention to me. And I thought to myself in a dreamy kind of way that maybe I had gone crazy. My whole leg felt cold, and I could feel my foot swinging and wet, as the man who carried me ran on.

Someone laid me in a corner of the schoolroom. It was total chaos in there, with people running frantically back and forth, trying to figure out where everyone was. I couldn't see Mama. I waited for someone to bring Luan and lay him next to me. Uncle Vizar must have gone back for him by now. But Luan didn't come. Perhaps he had been taken to the hospital.

Now my leg felt burning hot. The pain washed through me in waves. I felt very sleepy, but I kept my eyes wide open. When I closed them, I saw the explosion flash in front of me again, and I covered my ears to block out the screams that seemed to bore holes in my chest.

More and more people came into the schoolroom. Mama came for a minute and gave me a piece of bread. For some reason, I was so crazy that I threw it on the floor. Then I wanted it back, but it was too late. Mama was gone.

There were cuts on my face and arms, little ones. And there was a terrible pain in my hip. A deep, aching pain that was worse than my ankle. For hours I was crying and moaning, rocking my head from side to side. The whole side of my ankle and heel had been ripped apart.

Mama sat with me then. Carefully she picked a few bits of metal out of my face and arms. But I don't think she really saw me. Her eyes were big and dark as later she sat staring out the window above me. I didn't think she could take care of me the way she was, and that frightened me worse than anything.

"Mama?" I asked. "Mama? Where's Luan?"

She didn't answer.

A lot of people were crying in that school. At night it

grew worse. Mama lay on the floor next to me and sobbed all night. I didn't even know where Ilir was. He seemed to have disappeared into the confusion. Maybe he had to go help other families. Nobody told me anything. I guess they forgot to.

FIVE

The next day a nurse came and gave me an injection she said would help with the pain. She rolled me on my side and gave me a shot in the backside. It immediately made me very sleepy. I could feel my eyes begin to close.

I tried to ask her about Luan. Maybe she couldn't understand me, because she hurried away. Then I slept for a long time.

And, I think the day after, a Red Cross doctor came with two helpers, and they put me on a stretcher. The doctor took a big pair of scissors and cut off the whole leg of my sweatpants. Then he pulled the cloth away from the big patches of dried blood. It hurt. I screamed at them and told them not to. I tried to hit them with my hands.

Why had they destroyed my pants? It was April and cold. What was I supposed to wear?

Now I could see how swollen my whole leg was. Mama stood behind the medics, watching. Aunt Sevdie was there now. She held Mama in a bear hug with both arms.

The stretcher was narrow and made of canvas and smelled funny and musty. I think I lay on it for a long time. Mama disappeared. Then a nurse came again, and two women soldiers from the KLA. One of the soldiers held my hand. Suddenly, there was Ilir. Maybe I could get him to do something. I sat up. "Get Luan!" I shouted at him. "You stupid fool. Go get him."

Ilir shook his head. He said, "Listen, Zana. You have to go with the Red Cross to the hospital in Prishtinë so they can fix your leg." Then he cried and turned away.

"Wait! Where's Mama going to be? Does Mama know? How will she find me again?"

The two KLA soldiers picked up the stretcher and carried it outside. The brightness outdoors hurt my eyes. I was shocked to see how strongly the sun was shining. They loaded me into the back of a white van. Someone got in and sat next to me, but it was a foreigner, I could tell that right away. He was fat, like all foreigners.

"Are you from Switzerland?" I asked.

He smiled and patted my forehead. He didn't speak Albanian.

"Can you get my mother for me?"

Again he smiled. The van started up, and we bounced

down the lane to the main road. I lay back on the stretcher and felt the tears trickle down past my ears as I stared at the white ceiling.

Prishtinë Hospital was on the edge of town at the end of a long driveway and traffic circle. It was huge. I have no idea which building I was taken to. Inside, the walls of the hallways were painted a dull green, but the walls of the rooms were mustard yellow. In each room were three iron-framed beds, covered with sheets but no blankets.

I was put in a room with a man whose head was completely bandaged. Only his eyes, nostrils, and mouth showed. When I saw him like that, I thought maybe Luan had been brought here. Maybe a doctor had already operated on him.

A nurse came in. The name on her name tag was in Serbian.

"Can you ask and see if my brother is here?" I said, careful not to speak in Albanian.

She smiled at me and pinched my cheek. She gave me an injection on my sore bottom, and I fell asleep. Later I got X rays of my leg. I tried to explain that my hip hurt worse than my ankle, but they didn't seem to understand.

The next day many doctors came to look at me. One

was an Albanian. After the others all left, she came back and held my hand.

"Hi. I'm Dr. Dobruna, a children's doctor. I am so sorry about all this. But I want to be honest with you. Your foot is very bad. We don't have many supplies here in Prishtinë. So we will send you to Belgrade for an operation."

"To Belgrade? With only Serb doctors? *No!* Please don't. I don't care about my foot. Just leave it the way it is. Don't send me there."

She smoothed the hair off my forehead, just the way my mother did when I was sick.

"Don't be afraid. There are very good doctors there. I have a friend, Dr. Jankovic, who may be able to reconstruct your ankle so that you can walk normally again."

"But what about my family? How will they know where I am? And my brother Luan? Is my brother here?" I didn't mention Burim. I couldn't.

She frowned. "What village are you from?"

"Rezalla." Then I added, "My mother is going to have a baby soon. Maybe she needs help."

"What's her name?" Dr. Dobruna asked, taking out a little notebook and pencil.

"Shukrie Dugolli."

"Okay," Dr. Dobruna said. "I'll see what I can find out."

Then she left, and I was all alone, terrified of being sent to Belgrade.

All afternoon I stared out the window, wondering what would happen to me. I could see some low hills that surrounded Prishtinë, completely without trees.

After several hours, the sun was going down, turning the sky a soft orange. Dr. Dobruna came back. Again, she took my hand in hers. "I'm very sorry to tell you this, Zana. But your father and two of your brothers were killed in the attack on your village."

It was strange, but I actually felt relieved. I knew Luan had been badly hurt. And I guess somewhere inside I already knew he was dead. But I had to hear someone else say it out loud. I had to have someone tell me, or I couldn't go on. I had been stuck. If I had told myself Luan was dead, and he wasn't, I could never have forgiven myself.

I didn't cry. I only nodded. Dr. Dobruna sat with me for nearly half an hour, and then as the sunset faded from the sky and hills, she left. I stayed where I was, still looking out the window. Several faint stars pierced the dark blue sky.

Now I had the words to tell myself the truth. My father and brothers were killed in the attack on our home.

The food in Prishtinë Hospital was truly terrible. In the morning someone brought me a piece of bread and a small glass of boiled milk. It had been boiled so long that a thick coating of scum lay on top. I didn't drink it, and later there was only tea and no more food at all.

The man with the bandaged head had his wife give me a piece of chocolate and some cookies. The next morning I peeled the skin off the boiled milk and drank it, but I couldn't swallow the bread.

Later that day, they took me in the ambulance again. We drove all day, six hours north, to Belgrade, the capital of Serbia.

In the city, the streets were clogged with traffic. I peered out the window. There were lots of Jeeps and Mercedes-Benzes. The stores were full of clothes and books and CDs. We drove by a McDonald's, just like the ones in America.

Shoppers crowded the sidewalks. Young ladies wore high, fashionable boots and little leather backpacks and expensive scarves, maybe from Paris. Were those the same people who were stealing from poor farmers? Kicking old men? Killing fathers like mine? I stared at them. Didn't they know there was a war going on?

This hospital was smaller and much, much newer than the one in Prishtinë. It looked almost like a hospital I'd seen in TV shows from America. And I suddenly realized how little my family had and how poor we were. In Kosova, my mother had never even learned to read. I was sure that everyone in Belgrade knew how to read.

I was put on a floor for children in a room all by myself. Instantly, tired from the long drive and the endless pain, I fell into a deep sleep.

For breakfast the next day, I had orange juice and bread with a big slab of cheese. It was delicious and I wanted more, but I didn't want to ask for it.

Then a doctor came in. I read his name tag: Dr. Dusan Jankovic. He was smiling and looked right at me, waiting for me to smile, too. But of course I couldn't.

He asked, "Well, aren't you going to give me even a very little smile?"

I shook my head. Didn't he realize what had happened in our village?

"All right. Never mind. We are going to fix your ankle for you, okay?"

I nodded. "But you know what? My hip hurts worse."

"Really? Show me where."

I rolled onto my good side. He gently felt my hip, pressing with his fingers.

"You have quite a deep wound there. Probably a piece of shrapnel is lodged there, from the mortar shell. That's what all these little cuts on your arms and face are. Well, don't worry. You can have that taken care of later."

I looked at him. "My father is dead," I said. "And my brothers."

It was the first time I'd said those words. I wanted these Belgrade people to know what had happened. I wanted to tell him that I was not a terrorist and neither was my father. I wanted to tell him how good and kind my father had been, that they had no right to kill him or my brothers.

He looked away from me as though he was embarrassed. "I'm sorry," he said.

But I didn't believe that he was. If he was so sorry, why didn't he stop what was happening?

"What is it?" he asked.

I shook my head, tears filling my eyes.

"We'll operate tomorrow morning. But this repair job is a little complicated. Fixing your ankle may take several operations and a long rest afterward. It may be months before the wounds heal. You're going to be our guest here for a while. Eat a big lunch today. You could use a little energy."

But I didn't want to eat. I wanted to go home. I wanted my family back.

At 7:00 a.m., two orderlies wheeled my bed into the operating room. I was strapped to the table. A huge light hung over me. I looked around frantically for Dr. Jankovic. Before I knew what was happening, someone sitting behind me placed a plastic mask over my face so I had to breathe into it.

"Count to twenty," the voice said. "Come on."

I thought someone in the room said jokingly, "Terrorists can't count."

The room tilted sideways. The huge light went on, and I floated up and into it.

SEVEN

For two days afterward, I lay looking out the window at some old-fashioned apartments made of smooth gray stone. They had balconies. Sometimes people came out to hang their laundry. One person kept a little dog there.

My whole leg was wrapped in heavy bandages. Twice a day, the nurses gave me injections for pain.

On the third day, Dr. Jankovic came in. He had his hands behind his back. "Hello!" he sang out in a cheery voice.

I managed to smile a little. Even though I hadn't been very nice to him before, I was glad to see him.

"Sorry I couldn't stop by earlier. I was off for two days. How are you? Everything okay?"

I nodded.

"You know, I have a little girl at home."

"You do?"

"Yes. She's seven years old. I told her all about you."

I didn't answer at first. "You told her about the attack on my family?" I wasn't sure I believed him.

"Yes."

I felt something soften deep inside me. Now one Serb girl knew the truth. She knew the story about me.

"You told her my father and two brothers were killed?"

"Yes. And I told her about your injury."

Again I nodded. Speaking in Serbian wasn't that easy for me. I wasn't used to it.

"Look, I brought you something. It's from her."

From behind his back, the doctor brought out a small box of chocolates with a bow of red ribbon taped on top.

"Now I have to go. If you're in pain, remember to ring for the nurse, all right?"

"Thank you."

"See you."

He was gone. I opened the little box and gazed at the neat rows of chocolates. There were sixteen of them, two each of eight different kinds. I chose the one wrapped in gold foil to be my father. The one wrapped in strawberry paper was my mother. The big, dark square nougat one was Ilir. Burim was the green-covered pistachio, and Luan was the chocolate cherry. I was the mound of chocolate-covered coconut.

Lying on my good side, I lifted the gold-foil candy out of the box and set it on the bed next to me. I remembered my father saying, "Don't let them fill your heart with hate. Whatever happens."

Had he known somehow that I would end up here in Belgrade, all alone?

Although I could never tell Ilir or Ardi, I didn't hate Dr. Jankovic. He had told his daughter about me, and she had sent me a present. For the rest of that afternoon I rested quietly, looking at my family of candies.

That night, very, very slowly, I ate one of the chocolate cherries. Then I closed the box and hid it under my pillow.

EIGHT

I stayed in the Belgrade hospital for a long time. Weeks passed, and slowly I felt stronger. The nurses gave me two crutches. I practiced and practiced going up and down the hall until I could swing along at a fast pace. But I still couldn't put much weight on my foot, even though the swelling was going away.

The pain in my hip settled into a deep, familiar ache. It was there all the time. I tried to forget about it.

I wondered what was happening with the war. No one told me, and there was no TV in the rooms. I worried that maybe the rest of my family had been killed. Otherwise, why hadn't they ever come for me? But then I thought that surely the Red Cross had evacuated them someplace. And maybe Mama had had the baby by now and she was too busy to call.

Every day for three months, I thought these same things over and over. Once I heard the nurses talking out in the hall. They were saying that I might have to be sent to an orphanage in Serbia. If they did that to me, I would run away the next day. I would walk to Rezalla if I had to.

Finally, one day at the end of July, two Red Cross workers came. They said my mother and Ilir were back home now, and that my mother had had a baby. I wondered if it was a boy or a girl. I wanted it to be a girl.

A nurse came in with some clothes for me to put on— a pair of nylon pants, a green jersey, and a hooded sweatshirt that said DISNEY WORLD U.S.A. on it. Probably no Serb kids wanted it because of the letters "U.S.A."

She slid a big slipper over my bandaged foot. When she wasn't looking, I slipped the little box with my chocolate family into the front pouch-pocket of the sweatshirt to take with me.

"Remember, you're going to have to change that bandage often, and keep it clean," the nurse said.

"I will," I said. But how was I going to be able to pump and carry water while I was on crutches?

I looked around, hoping to catch sight of Dr. Jankovic at the nurse's station, but I didn't see him.

The medics put me in a wheelchair and took me downstairs in an elevator. I was scared when the two doors slid shut, closing us into the little box. We didn't have elevators where I lived. I'd never been in one before I came here.

The white van drove me all the way back to the village school in Rezalla. It took all day to get there, more than eight hours. We passed checkpoint after checkpoint, and when we got into Kosova, I was terrified that we would have to drive through fighting. Although the Serb police and soldiers were everywhere, with their automatic rifles drawn and ready, I didn't hear any shooting.

The medics took me into the school. One room had been set up as a nursing station, and the Red Cross workers left me there. Someone ran to get Ilir and Uncle Vizar's tractor to drive me the rest of the way.

Then Ilir and Ardi burst into the room, and Ilir picked me up. He twirled around and around with me, and I clasped him around the neck, crying. He smelled like woodsmoke, not like hospital disinfectant. Ardi grabbed my crutches and raced back and forth on them.

"Where's Mama?" I asked.

"Home. You have a new little brother," Ilir said. "He was born last week."

"He has a squeezed-up little face," Ardi added. "And spiky black hair, just like you."

"My hair's not spiky! Give me my crutches back, you big dummy," I said.

He handed them over to me.

"I'm sorry about your foot still being hurt. I thought it would be fixed by now. You can use my Nintendo anytime you want," Ardi offered. "Come on. The tractor's here."

I was home, but I couldn't get used to it. Our burned-up tractor still sat in the barnyard, but someone had taken the wagon away, fortunately.

Mama rested a lot, lying on the sofa with the baby in the cradle next to her so she could nurse him without getting up. His name was Hasan. He was named after my father.

Nothing felt right. The house was empty and quiet. I missed Luan's teasing and rude, silly comments, and I missed having Burim to help warm up the bed at night. Ilir was sixteen now. He and my uncle had to take care of both farms, so Ilir was out from early morning until sundown. Then he was so tired he rarely spoke.

The baby cried and fussed a lot. And Mama? It was as though she wasn't really there. Just her body was there. Nothing else. Sometimes when the baby cried, she didn't even rock the cradle. I came in and did it.

When it was time for dinner, she got up and cut us some bread and cheese. We ate the same thing every day.

Aunt Sevdie baked bread for us. Mama had to bring in water for the tea because I couldn't do it.

At some point, I don't really know when, I stopped

eating. I often felt nauseous, so I just stopped. I didn't go out much either. Why should I?

Without my father and Luan and Burim, we weren't really a family anymore. Anybody could see that.

Sometimes I got up on my knees on the sofa and stared out the window at Lena's house up the hill. Her father wasn't dead, and she could do whatever she wanted to. She wasn't about to be killed for being a terrorist like us. But she didn't come outside much either.

I was so angry with her. She had everything. A car, two living parents, new clothes, and one day she would study at the university.

All I did when I stared out the window was think angry, jealous thoughts. Her foot hadn't been destroyed. She hadn't spent over three months in the hospital all by herself, not knowing what had happened to the rest of her family.

And why not? Because Lena was a Serb. That was the only reason. And it wasn't fair. I wished something bad would happen to her so she would know how I felt, how my life had been ruined.

It was September now and school started, but I didn't go. I didn't feel like it. Besides, Ilir wasn't going either.

One day when Aunt Sevdie stopped by, she came into the living room and sat down in the chair where my father used to sit.

My mother didn't even get up from the sofa where she was lying. She reached over and passed Sevdie a box of cigarettes from the coffee table.

"No, thank you," my aunt said. "Shukrie, listen to me, this has got to stop. Look at your daughter. She's so pale and quiet. Her wound hasn't even healed. When was that bandage last changed?"

Mama sat up, embarrassed to be criticized by a guest. She didn't answer, but lit a cigarette instead.

"Look how thin she is," Aunt Sevdie said. "And why isn't she going to school?"

I knew one reason I didn't want to go. I didn't want the kids to stare at me or take my crutches. I didn't want Lena and her mother seeing me limp up and down the road.

"I have a new baby to care for," Mama said.

"Babies take care of themselves at this age. Here. Give Hasan to me." She pulled the cradle closer and rocked him.

"I've asked someone to come visit Zana tomorrow. Someone from the health station."

"What are you thinking? We don't need help," my mother said proudly.

"You can't let her sit in that corner all day, brooding. Besides, her foot should have healed by now." My aunt stood up. "The doctor will be coming tomorrow around four."

Immediately my mother sat up and looked around as though she had taken an energy pill. If the house wasn't spotless when guests came, the whole village would talk about her behind her back.

"Fine. If you think it will help," she said.

NINE

I was in my usual place on the sofa when someone knocked on the door the next afternoon. It was a warm day for fall, and yesterday my mother had gone on a cleaning binge, sweeping everything and making me dust all the furniture, which I did slowly and badly. I got up when the visitors came in, and went to the living room door to meet them.

To my surprise, one was Dr. Dobruna, from Prishtinë Hospital, the doctor who had told me I had to go to Belgrade. Behind her was a young man with blond hair.

I sat down. That awful time of the mortar attack came sweeping back, filling me with its fear and pain. I felt dizzy and closed my eyes.

"Zana?" a voice asked.

Dr. Dobruna took my hand, just as she had before. I opened my eyes and glared at her.

I was angry with her. Why had she sent me away to Belgrade? And now that I was back here, everything was terrible. My foot was still a mess; my father and brothers were gone. And now my mother had a new baby, and she couldn't even take care of me and Ilir anymore. Why was Dr. Dobruna coming here like this? Did she feel sorry for us because my aunt had told her how badly we were doing?

I thought she was going to give me a lecture and tell me to help out more around the house. But she didn't.

"We came to see how you are. May I see your foot?" she asked.

I nodded.

She began to unwrap the dressing. "I brought a friend with me," she said. "From Great Britain. This is Rob McDonald."

Behind her, the young man knelt down and looked at me. "Hi. Good afternoon. How are you?" he said in Albanian.

In spite of myself, I smiled at his British pronunciation.

"Did you meet my friend Dr. Jankovic in Belgrade?" Dr. Dobruna asked.

"He gave me some candy," I said. I still had the chocolates that I had pretended were my family.

"I knew he would be good to you."

She looked carefully at my swollen foot. There was a trail of pink scars. One long scar stretched up the side of my leg, where they had taken bone to repair my ankle. She felt my forehead.

"You're very warm. Do you think you might have a fever?"

"Yes," I said.

My mother came in with the tea tray and three glasses of tea. There was no lemon anymore.

"My hip hurts," I said.

"Really?" Dr. Dobruna asked. "When did the pain start?"

"I've had it since—" The memory of the explosion rushed in upon me without any warning.

Suddenly I burst into tears. It was really the first time I had cried for all that I had lost. And once I started, I couldn't stop. My mother began to cry as well, and put her arms around me. Couldn't she see one reason I was crying was that I had lost her, too?

After a little while, Dr. Dobruna said, "Okay. Here, Zana. You'd better blow your nose. So much has happened to you all at once."

I nodded, honking loudly into the hankie she gave me.

Gently, Dr. Dobruna rolled me over and checked my hip.

"Dr. Jankovic said it's shrapnel."

"Probably." She pulled up my pants and helped me sit. "It may be causing the infection. Now, tell me why you're not going to school. Couldn't your uncle take you on the tractor?"

"I suppose. But I don't want to see the other kids."

"Maybe you should talk it over with this friend of mine, Zana. You can call him Dr. Rob."

"Doctor? He's not a doctor!" I said. "He's too young."

He laughed. "You're right. I'm still in school. But now I'm working here in your village at the clinic. I help children with war trauma."

"What's that?"

"It means I want to come visit with you, so we can try to be friends. And maybe sometimes we can talk about what happened."

"You want to know? It's not just about my father. It's my mother. She's not the same," I said, glancing at my mother angrily. She looked away from me.

He nodded. "You've all changed a lot, most likely."

That was true. Ilir now had to work all day. Even I was getting old. I would turn twelve on October 20.

"And the baby cries too much. I hate him."

"Maybe you can help your mother with the baby," he suggested.

I got disgusted with him then and turned my face to the wall. What did he know?

They talked to my mother for a little while, explaining

that they would control my infection with medication for the time being. Then, to my surprise, Dr. Dobruna made me drink some tea with a lot of sugar in it. She said I needed to drink more, and I had to eat every day no matter how nauseous I felt. If I didn't drink, she said, my fever would get worse.

"Listen," she said, "we're not going to worry about school right now. First you need to eat and drink, and we'll bring you some medicine for that fever in a few days."

After they left, I returned to my spot on the sofa and stared out the window at Lena's house. What was she doing today? What had her family done when the village was attacked? Had her parents somehow found out that my father had joined the KLA? Had they told the Serb military? It seemed that someone had.

Suddenly I saw her come out with a basket of laundry, which she hung to dry on the bushes. Her hair was shoulder-length and light brown. Mine was black.

I tried to open the window so I could yell over to her before she went back in. I struggled with the sash, but couldn't make it budge. She turned and went back inside.

I sank down on the sofa and did what I did best now. I went to sleep.

TEN

Three days later, Dr. Rob was back with my medicine. If I'd thought all I'd have to do was take a few pills, it seemed I'd been wrong.

Dr. Rob said hello. Then he held up a small plastic bag of clear liquid and took my arm. He started to explain, but I stopped him. I knew all about I.V.'s from the hospital.

I sat very still while he inserted the needle into my vein. Then he waited patiently as the medicine dripped slowly into my blood.

"I went to Macedonia to get this medicine because there isn't any in Kosova," he said.

"Just for me?"

"Yes." He smiled at me. "Do you have a friend to play with?"

I shrugged. "I don't know. There's Lena. She lives next door. But she is a Serb. She was my best friend. But not now."

"When the soldiers came to your village, what happened to Lena's family?"

"I don't know."

"You didn't ask her?"

"No. Her father doesn't want us to be friends anymore. Neither does my uncle."

Dr. Rob nodded. "Did you eat something today?"

"Yeah. Some bread. A little egg."

"Good!" He smiled. "This afternoon you will eat some more."

Suddenly I was furious. Who had given him permission to tell me what to do?

"My father's dead! Don't you know that? And my brothers, too. Why should I eat? What difference does it make what I do? The soldiers can come back anytime they want to and kill the rest of us. I wish they would just do it and get it over with."

I thought he would be angry with me for yelling. I thought he would pack up his medicine and leave. But he didn't. He just sat quietly.

And then I started to cry. Finally I asked, "Will my leg ever get better?"

He opened his bag and took out a comic book. It said UNICEF across the front. Inside were drawings of some kids in cartoon form. It showed soldiers shooting at their houses. I flipped quickly through the pages until I came upon a picture of a boy in a wheelchair with no legs.

Was that what he wanted me to see? Angrily I tore the page from the book and threw it on the floor. He picked it up and smoothed it out, looking at the image of the boy with no legs.

"Is that what you're afraid of?" he asked.

I nodded, embarrassed now for acting like a baby.

"Okay. Listen. I'm going to do my best to make sure your leg is repaired completely. But right now we can't arrange for an operation. So that's why the first thing we'll do is try this special antibiotic by I.V. And if I have to, when I get the chance, I'll fly you to a hospital in England, where I'm sure they can help you. Do you understand?"

I nodded. He was being very nice. But I didn't believe him. He'd probably come once or twice and then get tired of our terrible life here and leave. That was what most foreigners did. But to be nice in return, I sat still while the rest of the medicine dripped down the tube and into my arm.

After he left, I went outside for a little while. I walked into the orchard, away from the wind. I wondered what Lena was doing. Did she worry that the soldiers might come back, the way I did? We no longer had my father to protect us. Now there was only Mama, or a piece of Mama, left.

I picked up a half-rotten apple, a soft green on one side and a damp squishy brown on the other, and I threw it as hard as I could in the direction of Lena's house, pretending it was a grenade.

Boom! I heard it explode in my head. I pretended that I could hear her family screaming in terror, frantically trying to leave the house.

I threw a second apple-grenade. *Boom!* I pretended that it killed her father, that he lay dead on their steps.

Then I heard my father's words again: "Don't let them fill your heart with hate."

If only the Serbs knew what my father had been like. They had killed the wrong man. But although he was dead, the Serbs had no right to make him disappear. If I kept his memory alive and remembered his words, his kindness, maybe my loneliness wouldn't be so unbearable.

My birthday came and went. No one mentioned it. Maybe next year I'd have a party. I wouldn't invite Lena.

Every few days Dr. Rob came with another I.V. bag, and we sat silently on the sofa while it dripped into my arm, leaving a soft, cool place where the needle entered.

One day he brought a banana with him. He took it out of his coat pocket, peeled it, and took a big bite.

"Would you like a piece?" he asked.

I wanted to say no, but found myself nodding instead. He broke off half and gave it to me.

"You know, sitting in that corner of the sofa won't bring your father and brothers back."

"I know."

"Sometimes, no matter how terrible the things are that happened to you, you have to get up and go on."

"Go on? I can't even walk. What if they have to amputate my leg? What if I end up in a wheelchair?"

"You won't. You have to help me fight this infection, you know. Right now, that's your job."

I didn't want to talk about it anymore. I turned on the television to MTV Belgrade. "Do you have any CDs?" I asked.

"Yes," he said.

"What's your favorite group?"

He laughed. "You wouldn't like them."

"How do you know?"

"I listen to techno, and a lot of crazy stuff. Iggy Pop."

"Do you like Cher or Mariah Carey?" They were Lena's favorites.

"Not really."

"Lena does. She has their CDs. And their photos."

"And that's because she's Serb, right?" he said sarcastically. "And her parents have money."

"Yes. No one will steal it from them."

He sighed and shook his head. I didn't want to talk about Lena with him. He would never understand our situation.

"Dr. Rob, what's wrong with my mother?" I asked.

"She's sad. And overwhelmed with the new baby and from the accident."

"It wasn't an accident."

"No. You're right. It wasn't. I don't know the right word for it in Albanian."

"You don't? Yes, you do. It's *lufte*. War."

He didn't speak for a minute or two. I looked at the top of his bent head and wondered what it would be like to have sandy blond hair. If I had blond hair, I would be beautiful.

"Listen, Zana, maybe this will all be over soon. There's going to be a cease-fire, did you know that? The Serbs and the KLA are going to stop attacking each other. The Americans are arranging it. That's good news, eh?" he asked.

That wasn't good news. Not to me. I didn't believe it would change anything.

"It doesn't matter who arranges it. They will never stop driving us out of Kosova. Just ask them. It's their destiny. Any Serb can tell you that. They won't let the Americans talk them out of it. Haven't you ever heard their songs about killing us?"

He looked sad. The I.V. bag was almost empty. Very gently he removed the needle from my arm and pressed down hard on the spot with a piece of gauze soaked in alcohol. Then he put a Band-Aid over it.

Finally he said, "Well, I don't agree with what you said. But it's okay if we don't agree on everything. The important thing is that we stay friends, right?"

A British doctor and I could be friends? I stared at him with curiosity. Was Britain full of people like this? Did he really think he could be friends with a crippled twelve-year-old Albanian girl? I nodded, to be polite.

He came on and off for nearly three weeks. And then there was no more of that medicine in Macedonia. But at least my fever was gone for now. And I did feel stronger.

ELEVEN

As winter began, there was supposed to be a cease-fire between the KLA and the Serb army. But every night on the news from Albania we heard reports that said the Serbs were bringing more and more tanks, weapons, and soldiers into Kosova. We didn't need the news to tell us. We could see this for ourselves.

Armored personnel carriers were everywhere. And Jeeps with machine guns on top. Every kilometer, it seemed, there were now large police barricades, where they stopped and searched Albanians.

One man from our village went to Prishtinë to try to get a visa for Switzerland. He wanted to visit his brother. He never came back from Prishtinë. His family believed he had been arrested and put in prison somewhere.

Little Hasan stopped crying so much. Now he liked to

lie on his back and wave his little toes in the air. Sometimes he grabbed his foot and shoved it in his mouth. Once in a while, Ilir would try the same thing, just fooling around, and Mama and I would laugh at him. I began to really miss having someone to play with. I even missed Luan's teasing.

One day in early January, while Mama was scrubbing the floors, I took my crutches and went over to Lena's house. School was closed because there was no heat, and I wanted to see if she got any great presents for New Year's.

I hurried up the lane and into their yard. They didn't have a cow. In their cowshed, they kept their car. Their front door was oak, with stained-glass panels on either side to let light into the hallway. The Gorans were rich. They had cousins in Pittsburgh who sent them money once a month.

Lena came to the door and her mouth fell open, she was so surprised. She hadn't seen me since the day on the bus last year. Then she laughed and threw her arms around me, crutches and all. She pulled me inside and closed the door.

"Hi!" I said in Serbian. No Serb kid would ever speak Albanian. "What did you get for New Year's?"

"Two CDs." She grinned. "The latest Mariah Carey."

"Anything else?"

"New jeans. A sweater. Nail polish. Want to see?"

"Sure."

She kept her things in several drawers in the tall wardrobe in the hall. She snatched her presents out of the drawer. The hallway was unheated, so we couldn't wait to get back to the warm kitchen. Lena put one of her new CDs in the player and started dancing, her arms up over her head, showing off her new moves from MTV.

"Come on, Zana," she said. "Dance with me."

I sat down, feeling sorry for myself. "I can't," I said.

"Yes you can." She pulled me to my feet. "Just move your hips and shoulders, and you'll be great."

I dropped my crutches and swayed to the music with her. Lena sang the lyrics in English at the top of her lungs.

After a few songs, I felt tired. Lena turned off the CD.

"We can dance later if you want. Look! I got lipstick and a hair clip. Sit still. I'll give you a makeover."

She twisted my long dark hair and clipped it to the back of my head, pulling a few strands loose around my ears and forehead. Then she put on the lipstick and handed me a little mirror. I couldn't believe how I looked!

"I look ancient! I look like I'm twenty-five."

"You look fantastic. Now do me," she said. She sat down in a chair facing me so I wouldn't have to stand up.

"This is fun," I said.

"Yeah. I really missed you. You know what, let's stay friends, okay?"

I didn't answer right away.

She grabbed the hairbrush and said, "What's the matter? You don't want to?"

I grabbed the hairbrush back. "Of course I want to. I'm just . . . scared, that's all."

"Oh," she said softly. "Yeah. I'm sorry about . . . everything."

I nodded. I was sorry, too. I finished her hair and was just starting to put the lipstick on her lips when the door opened and Mr. Goran came in. He stared at me and seemed about to say something—maybe that he didn't want me in his house.

Nervous, I dropped the lipstick on the floor, and the soft end of it broke. But he didn't say anything to me, not even hello. He walked quickly through the kitchen into the living room.

"Should I leave?" I whispered to Lena.

"No! Don't go. He's an old grouch. Who cares what he thinks?"

I giggled, and Lena laughed. And then we put glittery purple nail polish on our nails and blew on our fanned-out fingers to dry them. But I didn't really feel welcome after that, and when my nails were dry, I went home.

On February 1, my fever returned. And so did my overwhelming fear that now the doctors would have to cut my leg off for sure. I thought about it day and night. I got big dark circles under my eyes.

Mama went down to the clinic at the school, and they sent for Dr. Rob. Two days later, we got a message that he had left the country to take a little boy for heart surgery in Switzerland, and while he was there, he would try to get more medicine for me. He said he'd come in ten days at the latest.

I lay on the sofa and stared at the TV day and night. I didn't believe he'd get medicine for me, for one kid, when so many Albanian kids were sick and weak. Probably he'd never come back to our village. Why should he? There was nothing here, nothing for anyone.

The midwinter days crawled by. It snowed once, but the snow melted immediately, and the lane and farmyards were a sea of mud. The ends of my crutches sank into the soft ground, and I had to pull them loose with every step.

On Valentine's Day, I was secretly hoping for a surprise, a brand-new box of chocolates. Instead, that day Mama and Ilir began to argue.

"I joined the KLA," he said that night as we ate our bread and cheese.

"What?" Mama slammed the cutting knife down on the table. "Don't joke about that," she said angrily, but she kept her voice calm.

"I'm not joking. I'm serious."

"You can't go. You don't have my permission. Do you want me to lose all the men in my family in one year?"

"There's going to be another war. I can't sit home and watch while the Serbs blow us to bits. Is that what you want?" he argued.

I felt sick to my stomach and began to crumble my bread into little pieces.

"NATO will come save us. They know what they're doing."

"So does the KLA," he said proudly.

"Don't be foolish. The KLA is completely disorganized. Every other man says he is the commander. What kind of army is that? What kind of army takes sixteen-year-olds? I'll tell you!" she shouted. "A poor one!"

He glared at her and cut himself a huge piece of bread.

"Who will take care of the farm?" she asked. "And if you leave me and Zana and the baby alone, how will we survive?"

Suddenly it seemed my mother had come back to life after a long, long sleep. I was proud of her for standing up to Ilir.

"It's time for us to win our independence," he said finally. "Everyone needs to help. We've waited five hundred years for freedom from our oppressors. We can't miss this chance."

My mother sighed. I could see she was trying to be more patient now.

"We'll win independence through NATO. With only the KLA, we'll be destroyed in a war that will drag on forever. It sounds to me like you've been listening too much to Uncle Vizar. Well, let me tell you this: my sister Sevdie married a fool, a man who brags but does nothing."

"That's not true. He's in the KLA, you know."

"Oh, sure, I know. And when has he ever gone with them? Hmm? Where will you train? In Albania? A country full of bandits and Mafia? How can you train in those mountains? The Serbs have snipers and land mines everywhere along the border."

The baby started crying, and Mama went to get him from his cradle. Ilir got up and slammed out of the house.

I hurried to clear the table. I wanted to find out where he was going. I took Mama's long woolen sweater-vest from the peg by the door and rushed outside.

I thought he would go across the lane to my uncle's house. I was sure Uncle Vizar had helped him sign up. He should never have done that without telling my mother.

But to my surprise, Ilir was running the other way, down the hill to the orchard. I followed and hid behind a tree.

He hurried past the first few trees and then over to the right, where a fence made of woven branches separated our yard from Lena's. He hunched down and probed the ground with a stick, then started to dig at the earth. But he stopped, snapped the stick angrily in two, and strode past me, up the hill.

I waited until he'd gone back inside. Then I crept over to the spot, tossed my crutches aside, and began to dig. I didn't have to dig far before I felt the stock of the Kalashnikov. So this was where my father had buried it.

My first impulse was to take the gun and hide it where Ilir couldn't find it. But then I thought again. He'd know immediately that I was the one who took it, and he would be furious. He could always get another gun, anyway.

I didn't know what to do. I couldn't tell my mother about this. She was so angry already that I was afraid she might beat Ilir and that he might run away for good.

I covered the gun again, picked up my crutches, and went back to the house, making sure I brushed off all telltale signs of mud before I went in. If they wanted to know where I was, I'd tell them I'd been in the outhouse.

I headed straight for the TV. I didn't say a word to Mama about the gun. But I felt so weak and feverish that I didn't want to think about anything anymore. I lay down and closed my eyes.

TWELVE

When Dr. Rob finally came to the house in early March, I could barely get up. My leg felt warm, and it seemed swollen.

Dr. Rob unwrapped my bandage and swore in English, the way actors do in the movies. He sat back on his heels and stared at the blank TV.

"What's wrong?" I asked.

"I should never have gone to Switzerland. I should have come straight here instead."

My mother came in, drying her hands on a dish towel.

Dr. Rob stood up. "I'm sorry, but I can't treat her here. Not with her leg like this. She has to go back to Prishtinë Hospital, the sooner the better."

"No!" my mother said. "She can't go there. They've thrown all the Albanian patients out in the street. There are only Serb doctors working there now. She won't be safe!"

"She has to go. I'm sorry, but she's not safe here, either. If she doesn't start receiving very high doses of antibiotics soon, she could lose her leg, if not her life. The bone is infected again. She can take these pills that I brought for now. After I get her into Prishtinë Hospital, I'll go to Belgrade and arrange for her to be transferred there or, better, to England. I can get help in Belgrade from the British Embassy."

"I'm not going!" I yelled. "I hate those hospitals. I want to stay home."

Dr. Rob took Mama's arm and led her into the kitchen. I burst into tears and threw one of the pillows across the room. I was scared of going back in the hospital. I didn't want any more operations. I hated my leg.

Dr. Rob came back into the room, with Mama following him. He knelt down in front of me and took my hands. "I'm sorry, Zana, but I have to take you back there. I'll have you home again as fast as I possibly can."

"I thought you said you were my friend. If you were, you wouldn't do this to me," I answered.

I pulled my hands away and turned my face to the wall.

"You'll be okay, Zana. So, listen, I'll come back for you with a car, all right?"

"It won't be that easy," Mama said bitterly. "Not like

before. There are roadblocks everywhere. The Serbs hate foreigners as well, you know. How do you know they'll let you transport her?"

"I can manage it. I know I can. I'll see you soon. Bye-bye."

He zipped up his parka, grabbed his mittens from the sofa, and left. I stayed, not moving, staring at the wall.

Mama sat down in the armchair and sighed. "He's a very nice young man, but he doesn't understand our situation. The Serbs will never stop fighting us."

Hasan woke up and began fussing in his cradle. Mama untied the strap that held him in and picked him up to nurse him. I watched her from under half-closed eyelids. Her face looked very grim.

"This war will take a very long time," she said to herself.

When Hasan was done nursing, she buttoned her blouse and looked at me. "Come on," she said. "Get your coat on."

"I'm not going anywhere," I said, my voice rising in panic.

"You're going to help me get ready. Bring the cradle outside, and go get the shovel and the wheelbarrow."

In the kitchen, she began to fill plastic bags with flour, which we bought in huge fifty-pound bags. After I found the shovel, I came back in and helped fill bags with sugar and salt, while Mama poured oil into plastic soda bottles. I hobbled back and forth to the wheel-barrow, filling it with the food.

Mama put the cradle on top of the whole pile. Then she slipped on her coat and set off down the hill, away from the lane. I followed slowly, carrying Hasan and using only one crutch.

Mama went far into the orchard, where no one could see us from any direction, and then began to chop at the half-frozen ground with the shovel. It took us well over an hour to bury all the food.

When we were finished, she grabbed my shoulders and said, "Don't you dare tell anyone about this, no matter what happens. Not even Ilir."

I nodded, too frightened to speak, and we walked silently back to the house. Now I had two secrets, Mama's and Ilir's, because they didn't trust each other.

The next night, I woke up around 2:00 a.m. I propped myself up on my elbow. Across the room, Ilir slept soundly on the other sofa. Outside I heard the roar of a big truck engine, and men shouting and swearing in Serbian.

For weeks it had been on the Tirana news that Serb soldiers were terrorizing people in the cities of Pejë and Gjakovë every night—shooting a few Albanians and then driving up and down the streets all night, machine-gunning nonstop, while the KLA took over the roads in the countryside. But now the Serbs were here, here in my village. Where were our KLA guys? Why didn't they help us?

When the gunfire started, it sounded so loud I thought it might rip the windows out of the house. I heard the rattle of bullets shot into the air falling onto our roof like metal raindrops.

The truck engines roared as they struggled up our narrow, hilly lane. Their headlights bounced up and down in the tree shadows and on the wall of the living room.

Mama came into the room wearing all her clothes, even her shoes, and closed the heavy velvet curtains.

"Stay in bed, Zana. Don't go near the windows," she said. "There may be stray bullets."

"Why are you dressed?" I whispered. My heart was pounding rapidly. "Are they going to shoot us now?" I could almost hear the soldiers banging on the door. With every passing second, I wondered if this one was my last.

"No, no. They're just trying to frighten us. They're waving the Serbian flag from the Jeeps, that's all. If we stay quiet, we'll be okay." She sat down next to me and stroked my hair.

I was so relieved that Mama was no longer an empty

shell who rarely spoke. This new mother, the one who told Ilir he couldn't join the army, the one who had buried food in case we were attacked, who had tried to explain our fate to Dr. Rob, could take care of us, if anybody could. She had taken a little bit of Papa's calmness and stored it deep inside herself. I wanted to do that, too.

Ilir sat up now. "If the Gorans had any guts at all, they'd go out and tell those soldiers to leave this village alone," he said.

"We can't expect that," Mama said. "They want this all to stop—"

"Then they should stop it!" Ilir said angrily.

Mama didn't answer. She sat with me until finally the trucks and Jeeps drove away.

In the morning, Uncle Vizar came over to tell us that they had shot one of our schoolteachers in his front yard. He was forty-eight years old and had three children.

Later, his family buried him in the little graveyard at the crest of the hill where my father and brothers were buried. Everyone in the village went and stood silently around the grave while Uncle Vizar and Mehmet Bagu, the beekeeper, helped the teacher's sons fill in the hole.

I stared at Burim's and Luan's graves next to my father's. Burim's was so small. We had no money for headstones for the dead in my family. Instead, Ilir had cut three wooden markers and painted their names and the date they died in white paint. The letters were messy and crooked. Someday I would make better markers and maybe even plant some flowers there.

THIRTEEN

Every morning after the funeral, I woke up feeling tired. I felt worse and worse. My leg ached as it had before, especially deep in my hip. I didn't want to get up, but sooner or later, Mama made me. She made me take the pills Dr. Rob left. It was the best we could do. There was no way Dr. Rob could get back to us now.

Mama did her chores quickly and then turned on the TV. Then my aunt and uncle and Ardi would come over. All day long, the grownups stared at the TV, waiting for news. We saw the American Secretary of State, Madeleine Albright, and President Bill Clinton make speeches, telling the Serb army to leave Kosova and let the people alone, to stop killing them.

Finally, one day President Clinton and British Prime Minister Tony Blair said that if the Serbs did not stop the attacks on us, then in two weeks, on March 24, NATO would bomb them and then force the KLA to disarm. My mother cheered and leaped into the air.

"God bless President Clinton," she cheered. "President Clinton, I kiss you!" She threw him kisses.

My aunt and uncle laughed.

"Now let's see what Belgrade TV has to say about that," Uncle Vizar said, changing the channel.

How could the grownups be so cheerful? I was afraid. If possible, I was more terrified than before. Bombs? The Serbs would be furious, and they would take it out on us! Couldn't Mama see that?

Sure enough, Serb politicians on TV were outraged. "The Americans are sworn enemies of the Serb people. They are out to destroy us and have allowed themselves to be manipulated by the terrorist and separatist Albanians, who we all know seek to divide Serbia to form a Greater Albania."

I grabbed my crutches and went outside. It was March 10, 1999, and to me it was the end of the world. I knew my father would have understood that now our lives were in more danger than ever.

Slowly I made my way up the lane to Papa's grave. I let my crutches fall to the ground, and I sat down beside the lumpy mound of earth covering his grave and began to cry.

Bombs would fall here and destroy everything beneath them. Now Lena would hate me for sure. I didn't care about Serbs or Albanians or NATO. All I knew was that I was slowly losing my life. I felt betrayed by everyone and everything. I couldn't trust the ground itself. If a bomb fell on it, it could swallow me whole. The metal of a tractor could be twisted like paper.

A light wind swirled up from the wooded valley below, and with it a misty drizzle began to fall. I didn't move. I didn't care if I got wet.

Through my tears, I watched three speckled hens break out of some shrubs and scurry, clucking, for the nearest cowshed. Those hens were stupid. They thought the shed would protect them, but I knew better. There was no protection from war. I put my head on my knees.

When I looked up, I saw Lena standing in the lane, watching me. She was holding two daffodils from her mother's garden. I had a weird and dreamy feeling that sometime or other this had happened before, that she had brought daffodils to my father's grave.

But this time she stayed where she was. She didn't come any closer. She seemed afraid of me. Then she turned around and ran home.

I sat there until I felt numb. Then I went home, as well.

FOURTEEN

Before we knew it, it was March 23, the deadline for Serb troops to leave. No one did any housework or farm chores that day. Instead, all the neighbors came out of their houses and stood in the lane, talking—everyone except Lena and her parents and the other two Serb families.

It was obvious that the Serbs had no intention of withdrawing their soldiers or weapons. In different parts of Kosova, near Pejë, for example, they were going house to house, looting, burning, and even shooting people—while the whole world watched. Out in the lane, people said the Americans believed that Milosevic would back down after a week of NATO bombing. That was what had happened when NATO planes bombed Bosnia. After a week of that, Milosevic called for a cease-fire, and there were peace talks. Both Bosnia and Croatia got their independence, and that was what we wanted.

"Imagine," my uncle said, "a free Kosova two weeks from now."

But I didn't believe him, and neither did plenty of others.

The borders to Serbia were closed to outsiders, and the foreigners were all leaving Kosova. That meant Dr. Rob must have left, too.

"The fact that all the foreigners are leaving means NATO will bomb for sure, as soon as they get their own people out of here," Mehmet Bagu said.

Mehmet read a lot of newspapers that his son brought him from the shops in Gllogovc. I wondered what would happen to his bees when the bombs fell. Maybe they would all fly away to safety and never come back.

"Why do the Gorans stay here?" Aunt Sevdie asked. "You'd think they'd go someplace safer to wait out the war."

"They stay because they're informers," Ilir said bitterly. "They should all be shot."

"Ilir! Stop!" Mama said. "Watch your big mouth."

"He's too young to know that Albanians are informers, too," said Mehmet. "If you make threats like that, young man, you don't know who you are putting in danger. Maybe even yourself. I've lived through a war already. I know these things. If your father were alive, he'd tell you the same. Neither side is safe. In a war, everyone becomes an enemy. Do you hear me?"

"Yes, Mr. Mehmet," mumbled Ilir.

He used the respectful form of address for an old man, but barely hid his anger at being lectured in public by a neighbor. My aunt and uncle stepped aside to give Mama some privacy.

"Go home, Ilir," Mama said angrily. "Please excuse us, Mr. Mehmet."

Mehmet bowed graciously. Glaring at Mama, Ilir turned and went back to the house. I followed, determined to find something really stupid on TV to watch so I could try to forget about what was happening.

In the living room, I saw that Ilir wasn't around. Maybe he had gone to see to the cow. I found competition skiing on ESPN sports, and forced myself to pretend I was a champion skier in the Swiss Alps. It worked for a little while.

I lay awake for hours that night, listening for war planes and wondering if we would live until tomorrow. And when I stopped being so scared, I wondered about myself. If we did live, and NATO did come, what would happen to me? Who would ever marry me like this, crippled in one leg? I was no better than a piece of firewood that wouldn't burn. No good for anything.

• • •

My aunt came over early the next morning. She and my mother and Ilir sat in front of the TV all day, trying to find out what was going to happen. I couldn't stand to watch and went outside.

Some early spring flowers were blooming, and there were buds on the apple trees. I wandered across the lane to play Nintendo with Ardi, but I couldn't concentrate on the game. Why try to play when you might be killed at any moment?

Then my uncle stuck his head into the living room. He had shaved and put on a sports coat, as though today were a special occasion.

"Come on," he said, "both of you."

We shut off the TV and followed him back to my house. Mehmet was there with his two grownup daughters. Both their husbands had left weeks ago to fight with the KLA.

My mother was serving everyone tea, carrying the tray from person to person. I put a bag of pretzels and some dried chickpeas in dishes and brought those in, as well.

"We have to have a plan," Mehmet said. "Last time we were attacked, we weren't ready, and panic can be fatal."

"You can have a plan," Ilir said. "But I'm leaving to go fight."

I could see my mother was ready to yell at him again, but Mehmet raised his hand.

"Part of our plan must be to survive. No matter what happens, we can't let them completely destroy us as they did thousands of Bosnians. Ilir, it's too late now. With three men already dead in your family, you must stay and help your mother, the baby, and Zana."

"But if they find me, they'll torture me and kill me, whether I'm in the KLA or not," Ilir said, near tears.

My mother was crying, wiping away tears with the back of her hand. Uncle Vizar stared at the designs in the red carpet.

"Here's another thing. Zana will never make it to the border if we have to flee," Mama said.

"We won't leave Kosova," Mehmet said. "We must plan to stay together and hide in the woods. With NATO on our side, this war shouldn't last long. The best thing would be to put Zana and the baby in a wheelbarrow. So make sure you keep one by the door. Have a bag of food ready, and your boots. And matches to start a fire."

Then we all sat in silence, thinking about our future and wondering which of us would be left alive when the war was over. Suddenly Uncle Vizar got to his feet and left. One by one, everyone else left, too. And my mother hurried into the kitchen to make loaves of bread.

A little after six o'clock, we were watching the news from Tirana, but it mentioned nothing about the threat of NATO bombs. It did show U.S. aircraft carriers in the Adriatic Sea off Albania. Rows of fighter planes with swept-back wings sat on the huge decks. Ilir was impressed. Each aircraft carrier was surrounded by destroyers that had huge gun barrels pointed at the sky.

But that was it, and at six-thirty we turned off the TV. Moments later, we heard the roar of war planes streaking overhead.

Ilir leaped to his feet and grabbed my hands. I danced, too. And then we all ran out of the house. All the villagers had come out. Everyone was cheering and jumping in the air and hugging one another. Finally, after ten years of persecution and killings, the world had come to help us!

And then we heard a huge explosion. It was nowhere close, but still it shook the ground and vibrated in my chest. It was the biggest noise I had ever heard. It was a bomb. A NATO bomb.

"It's in Gllogovc," someone called out. "They must have bombed the police barracks."

Everyone cheered again.

Quietly Mehmet walked about the crowd, urging people to go home and stay inside.

"Bombs are very dangerous. Look how high those planes are flying. Those pilots can't tell who they kill," he warned. "We must protect ourselves."

Everyone gradually quieted down and went home. The electricity had gone off, probably so the bombers couldn't see any targets. So we sat in the dark and listened as another group of planes roared over us on their way to Prishtinë and then north to Serbia.

After that, the night grew quiet as a tomb. I thought about Dr. Rob. The medicine he had left was almost gone.

From then on, during the days, we prepared our escape and wandered around aimlessly. In the evenings, the electricity went out before the news came on, so we had no idea what was really happening. We simply sat in the dark, trying not to be scared, and listened for the planes.

FIFTEEN

April 2, 1999, was a cloudy day that threatened rain. It was the day that the Serb soldiers came again to kill us. An old man who lived at the top of the hill came into the yard. My mother and I had just finished cleaning the cowshed. We knew at once that something was wrong.

"They're here," the old man said. "They've already executed three men. Get your things and walk down to the school as fast as you can, and don't speak. Hurry, or they'll kill you."

And he ran across the lane to tell my aunt and uncle.

Ilir threw two blankets in the wheelbarrow, and my mother hid the bread under them. We pulled on coats and boots, and I got into the wheelbarrow, laid my crutches next to me, and took Hasan in my lap.

I was shaking all over, I was so terrified. Ilir seized the wheelbarrow handles and pushed us over the lumpy mud and down the lane. My mother, Ardi, my aunt, and my uncle were right behind us, and behind them were Mehmet, his daughters, and their little children, ages four, six, and eight. No one made a sound.

Lena and her parents didn't have to leave. They were safe.

Behind us, at the top of the hill, we heard gunshots. Mehmet paused and looked back. "They are burning some houses," he said in a low voice. "Don't stop. Think about saving yourself now. Think about nothing else."

We hurried on.

At the school, there was a large group of police, and we were horrified to see paramilitaries there as well. They were the killers, the torturers, the rapists, the arsonists, dressed in black shirts and wearing ski masks over their faces so we wouldn't ever be able to identify them for war crimes. If the paramilitaries were here, it meant the end of our village. These men were the butchers of Bosnia. We all knew that.

Mama picked up Hasan and held him close, afraid that they would torture the baby in front of us. Ardi edged closer to me. I took his hand.

They had already begun to separate the villagers, taking the men from the women and children.

"Men over here! Come on! Hurry!" one of the paramilitaries was shouting. He was huge, with big shoulders. His mouth was a gaping, roaring hole in the black mask.

One soldier took Uncle Vizar. Another soldier grabbed Ardi's shoulder and pulled him.

"No!" I screamed, somehow remembering not to speak Albanian. I held his hand tightly. "He's only twelve. Let him go!"

"Quiet, Zana! Don't!" Mama cried. She was afraid they would shoot me.

Instead, the soldier let go of Ardi and moved on. He took Ilir instead. Mama moaned and shoved her fist in her mouth.

"Don't show any fear," Mehmet whispered to Mama. "I'll stay with him."

Then Mehmet hurried after Ilir to protect him if he could.

"Hey!" said the big paramilitary, hitting Mehmet in the back with the butt of his rifle. Mehmet staggered from the blow. "Where are you going, old man? Did I tell you to move?"

And then, in front of us all, he shot him in the back of the head. Mehmet flopped to the ground. A dark pool of blood spread under his head. His daughters screamed.

I looked at my uncle to see what he would do, but he looked at the ground at his feet and didn't move.

"You liked that, eh, ladies?" the big one asked. "Get going. All of you. Get out. Go to Albania. Kosovo is for Serbs. Get out of here. You wanted NATO to save you? Go find them, then. Go find Bill Clinton, if you think he will help you."

The soldiers hurried forward and pushed the women and children into a column. Hasan and all the little children were crying. With Mama pushing me and Hasan in the wheelbarrow, we began walking away from the village, away from the road, following a dirt path that led only to the woods and beyond that to the high mountains of western Kosova.

I turned around and glanced back. The village men stood huddled in a group, while the big paramilitary paced back and forth in front of them.

The path dipped downhill at that point. The wheelbarrow bounced over the ruts and rocks so much that I could barely hold Hasan and keep us from falling out. I looked back again, one more time, and saw the paramilitaries beating one of the men. Then the hillside rose up and blocked them from me.

Mama set the wheelbarrow down and began to cry. Quickly another woman took the handles and pushed me and Hasan so that the soldiers wouldn't notice anything.

For two hours the soldiers led us through the woods

and hills. It was drizzling and cold. The rain felt icy, and soon my hair was soaked. Finally we came to a steep hillside covered with trees.

"Lie down. Everybody. Get on your stomachs."

"But what about the baby?" Mama asked in Serbian. "The ground is cold."

"Everybody!"

They began pushing us down with the rifle barrels. I got out of the wheelbarrow and lay down as well. I was sure they would shoot us all, and I began to cry. The children were crying, Ardi, too.

"Come on, kids," said one of the soldiers. "We won't shoot you. We only shoot terrorists. You don't have to worry."

They made us lie there all day without moving. I was shaking the whole time from cold and fear. My leg ached terribly.

From the village five or six miles away, we could hear faint gunshots, machine-gun fire, on and off for hours. As it started to get dark, the soldiers took the wheelbarrow and left us.

But we didn't move. We were afraid it was a trick, and that they would shoot us if we got up. Two hours before dawn, Mama got to her feet. She reached inside her blouse and gave us each a piece of bread she had hidden there. The rest of the bread had been in the wheelbarrow.

"Eat this. It will help. We'll freeze to death here. We

should start back in the dark. Come on, Zana. Try to get up now."

I would have to walk back. Ardi put his arm around my shoulder on one side, and Aunt Sevdie did the same on the other side. Mama carried Hasan, and we started down the steep, dark, wet hillside, stumbling and slipping as we went. Every time we slipped, pain shot through my leg, but I didn't cry out once. I told myself to be brave in memory of my father and Mehmet, and that was what I did.

We reached the village at dawn. We came up the hill from the back, not using the road that led to the school. The house at the top of the hill was now a cement-block shell. There was no roof, no ceilings, no furniture—just a smoking, blackened cell. And on the outside wall the soldiers had spray-painted a large, black Serbian cross. I could see the bodies of two men lying in the yard where they had been shot.

Mama began to run ahead, sure our house was gone, too.

But to our surprise, it wasn't. There it stood, just as we'd left it. And my uncle's house was all right, as well. But there was no sign of Ilir or Uncle Vizar.

"Maybe the soldiers didn't enter our house at all," Mama said hopefully as we climbed the front steps.

But the door stood wide open, and inside was a disaster. The furniture had been chopped up and torn apart;

the TV sat upside down on the sofa with the screen smashed in. There were Serbian crosses spray-painted on the walls, and bullet holes from automatic rifle fire.

But the worst part was the kitchen. All the flour had been dumped on the floor so we couldn't use it. The salt and sugar had been emptied, too. In the piles of flour were broken glasses and dishes, which had been mixed with the flour to make sure we had no food.

The soldiers didn't know that Mama had buried flour outside in the orchard. Mama cleared off the sofa for me and Hasan to lie on. Then she found dry clothes for us to change into and wrapped us in blankets. As soon as she could, she hurried out to get flour to make bread.

When she came back, she was leading Ilir by the hand. He and Uncle Vizar had somehow survived. Ilir was ghostly pale. One side of his face was swollen with a big reddish-purple bruise where the paramilitaries had beaten him. He sat on the sofa next to me and didn't move. His eyes were shadowy and didn't seem to have any color at all.

Mama got him some tea, and we all sat huddled on the sofa under the blankets while he told us what had happened to the village men.

"As soon as you left," he said in a flat voice, "the paramilitaries made us stand in a line while they looked us over. They kicked us and hit us with the rifle butts. The big one wanted to shoot us on the spot, but the soldiers wouldn't agree. Over their walkie-talkie, the soldiers got orders to take us to a house near the school, massacre us there, and then set it on fire. So some of them took Jeeps and went back to the village to get hay. They could then soak the hay with gasoline inside the house, and in that way burn it more easily.

"After those guys left, the others began to push us all into the house. Just inside, in the entrance, there is a staircase."

I started to cry. I couldn't help it.

"Well, we were told to go up the stairs. I was near the end of the line. One of the villagers began screaming, and a fight broke out. The soldiers started shooting people right there in the stairwell. Bullets were ricocheting everywhere. But I saw a closet by the front door. I opened it, and Uncle Vizar and I slipped inside and shut the door."

Ilir burst into tears. "From in there, I could hear everything. All the shooting and the men moaning. But it was chaos, and I think some others managed to escape and run for their lives."

Mama hugged him, rubbing his back while he cried.

"Soon the other soldiers came back with the hay. They dragged all the bodies into the living room, spread the hay on them, and lit it. And then they left. I could hear the roar of the fire from where we were hiding, but we were afraid to come out in case the soldiers were still outside. The entry was made of cement, so it didn't burn much, but after a while, the smoke crept into the closet and I began to choke from it. It was burning our lungs. So we had to make a run for it. We hid in the woods all night. Then I guess we came here . . ."

He didn't say anything else. I was so glad he was alive that I barely thought about the burning house and the men who died there. Mama kept hugging him and crying. She wouldn't let go.

Several hours later, Aunt Sevdie, Ardi, Uncle Vizar, and Mehmet's two daughters came over. They found some chairs in the kitchen and brought them in, clearing away some debris on the floor as they sat down.

"They'll come again," Mama said. "The soldiers. Of course they will. First they took the men. Now they will destroy the village. So tonight we must flee again. At least, our family will have to. They can't find Ilir here, or Vizar."

I was exhausted from the long walk home, the fear, the excitement of seeing Ilir alive, the pain in my leg, and I started to cry when she said we had to leave again. "Mama, I can't go." I knew I'd never make it.

Mama turned to the other women. "Stay here for a minute and watch my children. Zana must go to the hospital."

"No! She can't!" Aunt Sevdie cried, then covered her mouth with her hands.

Already Mama was pulling a heavy sweater over my head and gathering up my crutches. She left my wet parka on the floor.

"Come on," she said.

SIXTEEN

She took me next door to Lena's. We had to bang on the Gorans' fancy oak door for a long time. They were too afraid to open it. When at last they did, it was Mr. Goran standing there. He didn't speak.

"Please help us," Mama said. "Drive my daughter to the hospital. She's very ill."

He shook his head. "I can't. We'll be stopped. There's no way we'll make it."

"Yes!" cried Lena, pushing past her father. "We have to help Zana. We have to." She hugged me.

Her father clenched his lips and looked down at the floor, thinking. "Come in," he said.

Lena took my mother's hand and led us both inside. Her mother poured small glasses of Coke for us. I gulped mine down. It tasted delicious. I couldn't believe they still had Coke at a time like this.

"If I'm stopped for transporting an Albanian, who knows what they'll do—to both of us," her father said.

"She can wear my clothes. She can use my ID. Just tell the police, when they stop you, that she's your daughter and she's sick," Lena said.

My mother asked for a piece of paper. She wrote down the name of the Serb doctor in Belgrade who had helped me before. I saw that her hands were trembling.

I was horrified that she was sending me away like this after all that had happened to us. But I knew deep inside that she had to do it. I closed my eyes for a moment and pretended I was talking with my father. I knew he would be telling me to go, to speak Serbian, to be patient, to keep hoping. I knew Dr. Rob would be telling me it was my job to get well. I knew Mehmet would tell me it was my job to survive, that there were enemies on both sides and friends on both sides. I already knew that. When I opened my eyes, I hugged Lena.

"This is her surgeon, the one who repaired the bone in her leg. When you get to Prishtinë Hospital, give them this name and insist that you be allowed to telephone him. That way they will be sure to admit her," Mama said.

Slowly, Mr. Goran took the paper and read the name.

He nodded. "All right. But we should call him from here first. And then have him call the hospital ahead of time. That will work better. Here." He handed my mother a brand-new cell phone.

Mama took the phone into the kitchen to call.

"Go bring Zana some clothes," Mrs. Goran said to Lena, and she ran to the hallway wardrobe to get them.

Lena even brought me her New Year's hair clip and pinned up my hair.

My mother gave me a quick, hard hug. "Don't cry," she whispered. "Not now." And she hurried out, without looking back.

Lena's father went out to start the car. Lena slipped a little yellow flashlight into my pocket. "Don't forget me, Zana," she whispered.

A few minutes later, we left.

I was all alone in the orthopedic ward in Prishtinë Hospital, lying night after night in one of the iron beds. I never made it to Belgrade. The roads were closed. No relief agencies were allowed to enter Serbia. Every night I lay in the dark, without electricity, listening to the NATO war planes fly over on their bombing runs. There was no radio, no TV, no newspaper or books. Only the long, lonely days, and then the terrifying nights.

When bombs fell in Prishtinë, the force of the explosions shook the building and rattled the windows so hard I thought they would shatter. Sometimes I took out Lena's little flashlight and shone it around the room and across the cracks in the ceiling. As the bombs exploded, little bits of white paint from the ceiling fell on me like snowflakes.

The day nurse called me a terrorist. Even so, the doctor in the orthopedic ward called Dr. Jankovic in Belgrade. All the nurses followed Dr. Jankovic's orders and gave me my medicine. At first I was on an I.V. around the clock. But later they ran out of I.V. bags and needles, so I took pills, as before. Then the pills ran out as well.

The day nurse told me all the villages in Kosova would be destroyed, that probably my family had fled to Albania by now, and that was where I should go, too.

I lay there for weeks, not knowing what had happened to Mama, Ilir, and Hasan, or even what had happened to Lena. I kept the flashlight hidden under my pillow, just as I had the box of chocolates before.

And then, finally, on June 9, it was over. The war ended. I don't really know why. All the Serb hospital workers gathered in the hallway, getting ready to leave before international troops arrived. NATO had won the war! They were scared. I stood in the doorway to my room and watched while they talked about what to do.

SEVENTEEN

A few doctors stayed, but the nurses left with the Serb patients for a hospital in Nis, Serbia. I didn't know what to do or where to go, so I lay in bed and cried.

One of the doctors came by and said that in a few days the Red Cross would come for me. He said my village had been destroyed, and no one knew where my family was.

I didn't know what to say. I lay awake all night, worrying about what would happen to me next. I was still awake when the sun rose.

Somehow, it wasn't the Red Cross who came. It was Dr. Rob! He came on June 13 and found me there in bed, all alone on the fifth floor.

"Zana," he shouted, bursting into my room. I got out

of bed and threw my arms around him. He hadn't forgotten me!

"I looked all over the hospital for you. I'm here to take you home," he said. "Your family is fine. They're waiting for you!"

But the Serb doctor was right about one thing. My lovely village had been destroyed by the soldiers. As we drove up the long hill in the international-aid Jeep Dr. Rob had borrowed, I could see that each house, except for Lena's, was ruined. Shelled, burned, shattered. Not one stick of furniture left. The tractors were burned. The cows were shot. Some lay dead by the side of the road. Only a few chickens were left. There were no roofs except Lena's and those of the other two Serb families. The chimneys stood alone, pointing at the sky like branchless stone trees.

Dr. Rob stopped the Jeep in my yard. There was a large white canvas tent. The house was an empty shell. My mother came out of the tent, carrying Hasan. She nearly dropped him in her excitement.

"Ilir! Ilir!" she called. "She's back. She's alive. Dr. Rob found her!"

I grabbed my crutches and hobbled over to her as fast as I could. Ilir ran up from the orchard and hugged me, too.

"We thought maybe you had died, Zana," Mama said

through her tears. "We couldn't find out anything, except that you never made it to Belgrade. And Pristinë Hospital told us you weren't there."

"She wasn't in pediatrics, that's why," Dr. Rob said. "She was on a different floor, for bone injuries."

"How about the Gorans? Is Lena okay?" I asked, worried that perhaps her family had been punished for bringing me to the hospital.

"Of course," Ilir said bitterly. "Nothing happened to them. Look at their roof. It wasn't touched."

"Oh, Mama! Look at our house." I hobbled over and peered in the empty doorway. Inside was only rubble and blackened bits of charred wood. Absolutely nothing was left. I leaned against the wall to stop the dizziness I felt. The war was over, but we had nothing.

"What will we do? Where will we live?" I asked.

"Here." Mama pointed to the tent. "Everyone has to live like this for now. We have some things from the UN."

I lifted the flap and peered inside. Mama had kept it tidy. There were heavy blankets spread on the floor and three mattress pads, one against each canvas wall. Gently Mama laid Hasan on one of them.

"The well is working, and some of the chickens have come back from the woods," she added.

"Yeah. But the Gorans have a car. And a television, and money," Ilir said bitterly.

"Come on, Ilir," Dr. Rob said. "They're good people. They helped Zana, remember? They're not the ones who attacked your village."

"It doesn't matter to me if they did or not. All Serbs are criminals now. They did nothing to save this village. They must be held responsible for what they did to us."

"I understand you're angry, but you can't blame them. It isn't fair."

"Fair? How could you possibly understand?" Ilir said bitterly. "You're a foreigner. You have a place to go home to. Why are you here, anyway? Why don't you let us Albanians take over now? We know what needs to be done."

"Ilir! Stop!" Mama said. "Dr. Rob is our guest. Go bring some water."

Ilir snatched one of the plastic buckets that sat next to the tent and went off to the pump.

"Listen, Zana, I lost my job with the medical aid organization," Dr. Rob said. "I can't be a doctor here anymore."

"Why?" Mama asked in a worried voice.

"Because I took that little boy to Switzerland. I am supposed to be here to organize health care, not directly help the children. So from now on, I guess, I'll just have to be your friend."

He turned one of the buckets over and sat on it. I leaned against him and rested my cheek on his head. I wasn't sure what he meant. If he wasn't a doctor in Kosova anymore, did that mean he couldn't take me to England to fix my leg? I felt dizzy with disappointment.

"Hey! It's okay!" He gave me a squeeze. "Are you ready to travel? During the war, I went home to Britain and made all the arrangements for you to come for an operation. I took your X rays from Belgrade, and the doctors near my home said they can repair your leg without a problem. And while we're there, my parents and I will try to collect some money to pay for a new roof on your house, all right?"

Mama hugged him, and I hugged him, too. It was amazing that he had come back to help me. Even when they said I wasn't in the hospital, he didn't give up. He kept searching for me.

Someday I wanted to give him a big box of chocolates with a huge red bow on top.

After Dr. Rob left, I went down into the orchard over near the stick fence. The apple blossoms had fallen off the branches. The hole had been dug up, and the Kalashnikov was gone. I struggled up the hill and looked in the tent and the cowshed, but Ilir was nowhere to be found.

EIGHTEEN

I fell asleep during the afternoon. It was mid-June and hot in the tent with the sun beating on it. When I woke up, it was after four o'clock. I heard shouting up the lane.

I peeked out of the tent. There was a large crowd of people at Lena's house. With my heart pounding, I grabbed my crutches and hurried up the lane to see what was going on. I was shocked to see Uncle Vizar there, and Ilir with him. They were at the front of the crowd.

Lena's parents stood on the steps, facing everyone. I could see Lena inside, standing behind them. Uncle Vizar was holding a can of gasoline. And Ilir had the Kalashnikov. I felt sick, but somehow made my way through the angry crowd.

"Kosova is ours now!" Uncle Vizar was shouting. "It's your turn to leave. Go. There's your car. Go to Russia, if you hate Europe so much!"

"Or should we shoot you for what your people did to us?" Ilir yelled. "For the massacre at the house. For burning people. For shelling them." He raised the gun. "Do you feel brave for killing my brothers? They were children. Or Mehmet, an old man? You shot him in the back of the head! He was a beekeeper, not a terrorist. He gave you his honey. It's time you paid for these crimes, wouldn't you say?"

"Ilir, no!" I yelled, pushing to the front of the crowd.

I had felt those things, too, especially in the Prishtinë Hospital, when the nurse was mean to me. But I also knew that I wouldn't be alive if the Gorans hadn't helped me. I wouldn't let Ilir hurt the Gorans. I knew my father would have stopped him.

I dropped one of my crutches and grabbed the barrel of the gun. After all the terrible things that had happened, there was only one thing I felt sure about—friendship. Lena was my friend, and her parents, even though they were Serbs, had respected that. And Dr. Rob was my friend, and so was the doctor in Belgrade who had told his daughter what had happened to me and then made the doctors in Prishtinë give me medicine to fight the infection. And those things were just as real as the paramilitary madman shooting Mehmet in front of us all.

We had nothing now—no home, no clothes, no food. Family members were dead. Neighbors were dead. My brother was filled with anger and hatred, following my uncle's path instead of my father's. Ilir had let the soldiers and paramilitaries fill his heart with hate. I couldn't let him be so influenced by Uncle Vizar, who I knew was nothing but a coward. He had left Luan behind because it was easier than trying to save him.

"Don't do this. Lena is my friend, Ilir," I said. I let go of the gun barrel and climbed the steps to stand with her parents at the top. I stood there staring at my neighbors. I didn't really know what to say. So I decided to be quiet and just look at them, hoping they could see what they were turning into.

"Zana! Get down from there!" Ilir shouted.

"No, I won't," I said. "Think about Papa. What would he say if he saw this? What would Mehmet say?"

I knew the villagers wouldn't harm me, because of my injury. In a way, in their eyes I was protected by what I had endured. I had survived against the odds, and they knew it. They wouldn't be the ones to kill me now.

Then Lena came out of the house and stood next to me, and we held hands. I was wearing the clothes she had given me in April.

"Hey! Lena, look," I whispered. "I still have this." I showed her the little yellow flashlight. And she smiled.

"Are you okay?" she asked.

"Yeah." We waited.

My uncle turned around and hurled the can of gasoline into the lane. He swore and walked off. Ilir followed him. The crowd began to drift away. The terrible moment was over.

Very early the next morning, I heard someone outside the tent, whispering my name. I crawled out through the flap. It was Lena.

The sun was just coming up, turning all the leaves a soft yellow-green. Little apples were already growing.

Lena's car stood in the lane, packed to the roof. Her parents were sitting in the front. The engine was running.

"You're leaving?" I asked.

She nodded. "I came to say goodbye."

I hopped over to the car with her. "Please don't go."

"We have to. What if that crowd comes back?" Lena asked. "You can't protect us forever, Zana!"

"I want to thank you for yesterday," her father said.

"That's okay." I didn't know what to say.

"But we can't stay here now," he said. "We'll go to Montenegro for a while. I have a cousin there we can stay with."

"Zana, listen. We'll always be friends, okay? It's not so far," Lena whispered. "I'll see you again."

I nodded. She kissed my cheek, and I kissed hers. She got into the backseat, filled with quilts, clothes, and pots, and they drove away.

I stayed right there and watched their car make its way down the long hill from our village. I closed my eyes tight, clutched the little flashlight, and wished that I'd see Lena again. But when I opened my eyes and turned and saw our shattered house beside me, I knew I was going to have to be patient.

The first thing, as Dr. Rob said, was to fix my leg.

In 1994, from the safety of my home in Maine, I watched television coverage of the war in Bosnia. I was horrified by what the violence did to people's lives. I felt especially concerned about the children who were caught up in the brutal ethnic conflict. Anxious that the war might spread from Bosnia to Kosovo, that year I began the first of many visits to the children of Kosovo, going to schools, talking with parents, spending time in the villages. Later, in 1999, I visited refugee camps in Albania and Macedonia.

This is the story of one family I became close to from the Drenica farming region, west of Pristina. They suffered in many of the same ways as Zana Dugolli's family, only it was a boy, not a girl, who survived a mortar attack that killed his father and two siblings and left him with an injury just like Zana's. But there was also a real Dr. Rob. After the war, "Dr. Rob" took the whole family to England so they could be together while doctors successfully repaired the boy's leg.

Needless to say, I do not have a political solution to the complex problems of the former Yugoslavia. But I do know that until there is true peace in the region, I will continue to work with human rights organizations to help all children there.